The Avenging Ranger

CONRAD G. HOLT

A Black Horse Western

ROBERT HALE · LONDON

© Philip Harbottle 2002
First published in Great Britain 2002
Based on a short story by John Russell Fearn

ISBN 0 7090 7154 X

Robert Hale Limited
Clerkenwell House
Clerkenwell Green
London EC1R 0HT

Typeset by
Derek Doyle & Associates, Liverpool.
Printed and bound in Great Britain by
Antony Rowe Limited, Wiltshire

1

The stagecoach was rumbling along the rocky trail that led to the small Texas town of Eagle's Bend, some twelve miles distant. Behind it trailed clouds of dust, shimmering in the blazing sunshine.

The driver was giving his full attention to the snorting horses as they neared a bend in the trail around the mountain foothills, where large boulders and rocky outcroppings afforded possible cover for both men and horses.

Alongside him, his eyes slitted in concentration on the trail ahead, his ramrod companion gripped his rifle more tightly. Since they were carrying a box of gold as well as a passenger, he was taking no chances on a possible ambush.

'Hold it!' the ramrod snapped suddenly, as they rounded the bend. 'Up ahead, lyin' at the side of the trail there. By thunder, it's a man!'

The driver clamped on the brake and jerked at the reins, and the panting horses reacted amidst an increased creaking of springs and jangling and squeaking of leather harnesses. From inside the coach came muffled cries of protest as the passenger was presumably jerked from the seat and flung across the carriage.

The body of a man lay in the dust, perhaps twenty yards ahead. He was lying face down, one arm outflung, the other twisted under his body. A short distance to one side of him, a saddled horse was nibbling at some sparse vegetation.

With a final screeching sound, the iron-bound wheels skidded to a halt in a cloud of dust.

'Looks like he's been thrown from his horse,' the driver said. 'He ain't movin'. Mebbe hurt bad – or dead. I'd better take a look. . . .'

'OK,' the ramrod muttered. 'But I'm keepin' you covered . . . just in case.' The driver clambered down and hurried forward to the unmoving figure.

He dropped to one knee and gently turned him over. Even as he noticed with a shock that the man's face was hidden behind a mask, he felt a sharp pressure in his stomach.

'Take it easy,' a harsh voice whispered. 'Unless you want a bullet in the guts!' The driver hastily glanced down to find that the apparent 'corpse' was very much alive, and holding a gun in the hand that had been hidden from view.

'Don't stand up,' the rasping whisper continued. 'Tell your friend to come down here an' lend a hand. Try warnin' him an' you're dead!'

The ramrod was now standing up in the coach, his rifle levelled. He could not properly see the fallen figure, hidden as it was behind the stooping driver.

'Well?' he called. 'How is he?'

Sweat beaded the driver's brow with the sick realization that he was very close to death if he disobeyed the man holding the gun on him.

'He's – he's hurt bad,' he said, without turning round. 'I need you to give me a hand to stop the bleedin'.'

'Wise man,' the gunman whispered approvingly. 'Now keep it buttoned if you want to go on livin' . . .' The driver continued to sweat, his mind now racing into a higher gear.

The ramrod had dismounted from the coach, and came forward, still gripping his rifle. Slowly, the gunman sat up, carefully keeping out of the ramrod's line of sight. He moved the gun from the driver's body, preparatory to covering the approaching man.

As soon as the gun barrel was removed from his body, the driver reacted. He brought an arm down in a swinging motion, knocking the gun further away from him and simultaneously flung himself to one side.

'*Gunman!*' he yelled. 'Look out —!'

Instantly the ramrod swung up his rifle. A shot crashed out.

The ramrod toppled forward on to his face in the dust. There was a bloodied hole in the back of his head. He had died before hitting the ground, a bullet in his brain.

As the driver scrambled to his feet, he saw that two other figures had emerged from behind rock cover to the rear of the coach. Obviously the whole thing had been a set-up. One man was striding towards him, his Colt still smoking in his hand. The other was leaning through the coach window, his own gun threatening the passenger – already badly dazed by the earlier abrupt stop – into cowed submission. Both men wore bag-masks over their heads, with large slits cut out for their eyes.

The first masked gunman had now regained his feet, and was dusting himself off with one hand. His other hand held the gun unwaveringly on the terrified driver.

'Not such a smart move,' the harsh voice said, no longer whispering. 'You gone an' got your pardner killed. Needn't have happened if you'd stayed smart. We've only come for the gold you're carrying.'

'OK, I'll take over from here.' The voice of the man who had fired the shot was less guttural, even educated. 'You,' he waved his gun at the now submissive driver, then swung it in the direction of the coach, 'get back up on to the stage, and throw down the box of gold we know you're carryin'. Do that, and we'll let you and your passenger go on livin'.' He laughed. 'We'll even let you complete your journey to Eagle's Bend.'

'What – what about Jake?' the driver stammered, glancing uneasily at the ramrod's dead body sprawled in the dust.

The gunman shrugged. 'Up to you. You can either pick him up and carry him back to the coach with you . . . or leave him here for the buzzards to feed on.'

To Evelyn Ward the journey had been one of breathtaking interest. It compensated her for the dust and heat of the trail. There had been – and still was – so much for the eye to see on the hundred-mile trip from Austin to Eagle's Bend. At this very moment the Overland Stage was rattling and bouncing its way along the sun-drenched trail. It was high noon and at the time of year when the deserts and mountains of the West are ablaze with colour.

Alone now in the corner of the stage – her other travelling companions had departed at different points along the route – Evelyn Ward smiled as she gazed out upon the Apache-plumes and dancing lilac of the loco weeds sweeping up in multi-hued carpets over the mountain sides.

Sombre, impersonal against the cobalt blue heaven, they reared like sentinels guarding the narrow trail through which the stage now plunged.

Suddenly, as if they were in another world, the sunlight was blotted out by the mountains, the blazing heat took on a chill. Then, completely unexpected, came two revolver-shots. Grinding and rattling the stage jerked to a standstill. There was a brief intense quiet broken only by the clinking of the team's bridle. A voice, sharply authoritative, spoke.

'OK, sling down that box! An' hurry up! We haven't got all day to hang around.'

Puzzled, trying not to feel alarmed, Evelyn edged her head round the open window and looked outside. Three horsemen, all of them disguised by bag-masks over their heads with holes cut for eyes, were training their sixes on the two men on the stage. Above Evelyn's head there was the scrape and rumble of a box being dragged. Then it crashed suddenly into the dust at the side of the trail and lay there. 'Right!' the voice commented again, and Evelyn saw that it belonged to the centremost man in the trio, carrying two guns whereas his companions only carried one apiece. 'Now let's see what else you've got.'

He neck-bridled his horse and jogged forward. Evelyn stared at him fixedly, striving to discover what kind of face lay behind the bag-mask. Failing, her eyes dropped from the glitter of his eyes to the guns. They were ordinary six-shooters; that much she knew. One of them, though, had a deep notch scored across the barrel as though at some time a bullet had ricocheted from it.

'Where're you heading for, miss?' the bandit asked. Evelyn did not reply immediately. She was trying to memorize the voice. It was fairly educated; certainly not the rough tongue of a gunhawk cowpuncher.

'I'm – I'm going through to Eagle's Bend,' she answered at length.

'Yeah? Why?'

'I've got a job there – schoolteacher. The education authority in Austin got it for me. It's they who've sent me . . . And I haven't got anything valuable if that's what you're thinking!'

'I wasn't thinkin' anythin' of the sort.' There was a sound rather like a laugh. 'I was just figurin' that you're as pretty a picture as any I've seen around this hell-fried country in some time.'

Evelyn looked away indignantly – and had she but realized it the action made her look all the prettier. She had waved black hair and violet-blue eyes, an almost Irish combination, to which was lent softly bloomed cheeks and straight features. Whatever else he might be the outlaw was a good judge of looks.

'All right,' he said abruptly. 'Get on your way. And sorry you were troubled, miss,' he added cynically.

His gun exploded deafeningly and the stage jolted forward again. Evelyn relaxed in the seat, frowning – wondering. She had not detected anything beyond a notched gun. She might of course recognize the voice again. Doubtful if she could recognize the man's figure. Seated as he had been on a horse it had been difficult to judge his height. His shoulders had been broad and strong.

The stage continued the remainder of the journey at a pace that nearly shook the life out of the girl, thundering and rattling into the sprawling township of Eagle's Bend some twenty minutes later. It stopped outside the sheriff's office instead of going on to the usual halt, and Evelyn watched the two drivers climb down into the dust and hail a big man standing at the tie-rail.

'Hey, Sheriff, there was a hold-up ways back down the trail! Didn't even git the chance to use our guns. Three lobos in bag-masks got us hogtied!'

Evelyn heaved her aching body out of the corner seat, pushed open the stage door and climbed outside. She stood watching the little knot of men and women gathering as Sheriff Jim Padgett listened to the drivers' story.

'So they got the gold, huh?' he asked finally, biting on his cigar.

'All of it! Ten thousand dollars' worth! I don't have to tell you it was being brought to the bank here from Austin, Sheriff. You were the one as arranged things, bein' the law around here.'

'Yeah, I did. That's right.'

Sheriff Jim Padgett stood ruminating for a moment. He was a big, square-built man in a black suit and sombrero and sporting a shoestring tie. Some folks liked him; plenty didn't. His badge of office gleamed on his wide expanse of vest.

'Okay,' he said grimly. 'Come back into the office here and I'll take it down in writin' —'

'But there ain't time for that! We need a posse right now to chase these gunhawks —'

'No, we don't. Can't get at things that way. A little strategy is called for, I reckon. Come on in here . . . .'

The sheriff and drivers vanished behind the screen door of the office. Evelyn looked about her somewhat helplessly. Some lounging cowpunchers eyed her with naked approval. Finally she signalled rather diffidently to a tall, soldierly-looking man in shirt-sleeves who had been listening to the story of the hold-up.

'Er – I hope you won't mind . . .' Evelyn hesitated. 'But would you get my box down for me from the top of the stage here?'

'Why, sure I will, miss!' With a genial smile the man vaulted up with surprising ease considering his years, pulled forth the box she indicated and then held on to it as he stood beside her.

'Goin' far?' he asked. 'This is a heavy box for a girl like you to be carryin'.'

'I suppose it is. It's got a lot of books in it . . . I'm going to teach in the school here. My name's Evelyn Ward.'

The elderly man nodded. Evelyn noticed he was a square-faced handsome man of perhaps sixty, with the tan of sun burned into his skin.

'I'm Fletcher James, editor of the *Eagle's Bend Gazette*,' he explained. 'Glad t' make you welcome, Miss Ward. Where are you stayin'?'

'I was told Ma Granson's would be the best place – wherever it is.'

'You couldn't do better.' James nodded down the dusty street towards a rather taller building among the shacks, bungalows, and stores. 'That's it – there, only roomin'-house in town, outside of the Grey Pearl Saloon which does service for a hotel. Ma Granson'll be glad to get you. I hear she isn't doing so well for money or boarders. Don't get many of those sort of people in this town, I reckon.'

They had been walking slowly down the street whilst talking. Evelyn kept her eyes on the rather shabby front of Ma Granson's rooming-house. It had a dilapidated, poverty-stricken look about it.

'Say, Miss Ward . . .' Fletcher James stood beside her as she knocked on the front door of the place. 'I'm the editor of the local paper, as I told you – and you were on that stage. Can you tell me anythin', apart from what I heard when the boys reported the hold-up to the sheriff, which might help us get the robbers?'

Evelyn reflected and then shook her head. 'I'm afraid I can't, Mr James . . .' She thought of the notched six and then decided it hardly constituted evidence worth having, not to a newspaper anyway.

'Pity,' James said, sighing. 'That's the second hold-up and gold-robbery in the past few months – each time on the stage between here and Austin. Sheriff Padgett's kind of leery of sending out a posse. Thinks it might make him look foolish when he doesn't get any results. Today's robbery makes it that altogether nigh on twenty thousand dollars in gold has been stolen. I reckon it's high time a real lawman came over to look into this. Can't seem to get any worthwhile action out of Padgett.'

'He knew the gold was coming, didn't he?' Evelyn asked, thinking.

'Sure he did – an' so did I. He told me so I could print the news. I shouldn't't've. Somebody knew there was a haul worth taking – and took it! As for the sheriff, it's only his job to keep guard over that gold once it gets into his town; if it vanishes before then he can't be held responsible. I —'

Fletcher James broke off as the door opened and Ma Granson stood there – wide, genial, but tired-looking. She had greying hair and welcoming blue eyes.

'Afternoon, Mrs Granson,' James greeted her; then

with a nod to Evelyn, 'I'm leavin' you in safe hands, Miss Ward. See you again, I hope.'

'And thanks,' the girl said, smiling. Picking up her box she entered the hall of the rooming house. Here again the sense of struggle against poverty became noticeable.

'Naturally you're Miss Ward?' Ma Granson gave a smile as she closed the door. 'I got the letter from the education people in Austin an' everything's fixed up for you. I hope you'll like it here. You're sure welcome anyroad.'

Evelyn shook hands and gave a faint smile.

'Tell you better whether I like it or not after I've been here a while. Right now I'm forming the impression that I'd rather be back on my dad's ranch in North Point.'

'I can understand that,' Ma Granson sighed. 'Eagle's Bend ain't much of a township – grown up out of a gold-rush. But it seems to hold its own purty well. I only wish . . .' She became transiently wistful and then shrugged. 'I was goin' to say I only wish I had more board-ers, but a youngster like you don't want to be hearin' my troubles, I reckon. Come on this way an' I'll show you your room.'

2

When she had freshened herself up from the trip and had a meal Evelyn set forth to begin orientating herself with the township. She was not due to commence her activities as school teacher until next day and so, definitely curious, she started an exploration which lasted her all evening.

In this time she failed to discover anything exciting. Eagle's Bend was the same as any other remote Western town – straggling, full of false fronts, dust, buckboards, cowpunchers, with ranches amidst the blaze of Nature outside the immediate town. The school, her focal point of interest, was little more than a large-sized wooden cabin, provided – like the Eagle's Bend church – with a solitary bell in a tiny little bell house . . .

She was returning to Ma Granson's in the late evening, walking through the primroses and whispering bluebells that spread in an endless carpet outside the town, when the rustle of feet behind her gave her pause. What she saw in the dying light did not impress her. A tall, travel-smeared cowpuncher – in fact little more than a hobo – was only a few feet away, advancing as she stood still.

'Miss – have you a minute . . . ?'

Evelyn tightened her lips, stood slim and subtly curved

in her thin frock against the amber and magenta of the sunset. The hobo came to her side and it was his size that disconcerted her. He seemed nearly six feet three with very wide shoulders and the neck of a prize ox. A battered sombrero was pulled low down over his dark, swarthy features. A sweat-stained shirt, dusty breeches, and worn thigh-boots made up the rest of his attire.

It was too dark to see his features or eyes. The only thing that gave Evelyn any feeling of relief at all was that he was not carrying a gun.

'Sorry to be botherin' you , ma'am,' he said slowly, in a deep husky drawl. 'I'm just a-wonderin' if you can tell me where I might bunk in this here town.' He jerked his head vaguely in the direction of Eagle's Bend, with its strings of lamp-lights.

'It surprises me a man of your type *needs* a place to bunk,' Evelyn answered briefly. 'I should think you'd do all right in a mesquite thicket.'

'I know I ain't lookin' too good with this dirt on me, ma'am – but I've come a long way, jumpin' a cattle train. I've a guy to see in Eagle's Bend here an' I likes to behave respectable as far as I can. You look like a lady who'd know th' best place for takin' a hobo like me.'

'All I can suggest is the Grey Pearl saloon. See the owner – I don't know his name because I'm new to this town myself. I expect he'll be able to fix you up.' Evelyn turned away into the twilight. The big fellow kept up with her.

'You don't mean that you live in the saloon yourself, do you ?'

Evelyn glanced up at his gloom-ridden features. 'What's it got to do with you where I live?'

'Nothin' – only I reckon a gal like you'd know all th' nice places t' sleep. I might like the same place.'

'I'm sorry,' Evelyn answered him calmly. 'I can't pass on the name of my rooming house: my landlady wouldn't thank me to bring in a trail-hitter like you. If you find the place for yourself it's none of my business. Now will you please let me walk by myself?'

'Sure!' There seemed to be grim amusement in the voice. 'Though why a gal like you should want to walk by herself is somethin' I can't quite savvy.' Deliberately Evelyn turned away – and to her inward relief the massive hobo made no attempt to force himself on her again. She had a dim vision of him in the twilight striding away towards the town, then she went on her way. When she entered Ma Granson's and went through into the dining room for supper she met two other boarders for the first time – and was unimpressed.

They were a cattleman and his wife, both of them middle-aged and stodgy.

There was still another person at the table, however – a man of perhaps twenty, broad-shouldered, good-looking after a fashion, with blond hair and blue eyes. It was the weakness of his chin that just couldn't escape notice.

'Enjoy your walk around, Miss Evelyn?' Ma Granson asked, as she ladled out the supper on to plates.

'Ye-es – but I'm afraid it's confirmed me in my opinion that I'm not going to be happy here,' Evelyn answered, taking the plate of hash and regarding it in vague distaste.

'Oh, Eagle's Bend isn't so bad when you get used to it,' the young man said. Evelyn looked at him sharply. Funny thing, but his voice sounded almost like that of the hold-up man she had encountered that noon. Almost like it.

Somehow it was less deep, though. Unless perhaps the bag-mask had muffled it a little and . . .

Evelyn gave herself a little shake. This was getting ahead of herself, letting her imagination run riot. She looked away, but was aware of the blue eyes watching her fixedly.

'This is my son Joe,' Ma Granson said, waving a hand to him. 'You've not met him properly yet. . . He knows a thing or two does my Joe. Eddicated himself he has – even if it's gotten him no further than the clothing store in Main Street so fur.'

'I'll do better – as I go on,' Joe observed complacently, his eyes still on Evelyn.

'Glad to – to know you, Joe,' the girl said, hesitating.

'Thanks,' he acknowledged, and gave an insolent grin. 'You are a pretty good addition to this dump, let me tell you. I spend my days sellin' clothes and come home to this ruin. It doesn't give a feller much ambition. But from now on it'll sort of be different . . .'

'Will it?' Evelyn asked him coolly.

He got up from the table. 'Sure will!' he confirmed. Then he turned to his mother. 'I'm goin' down town, Ma, for a bit of poker with the boys before turning in. See you again, Miss Ward.'

Evelyn watched him leave the dining-room, twin-guns slapping low down on his strong thighs. Her mind went back to the voice of the hold-up man, to her instinctive dislike of Ma Granson's son, and . . . She made a bothered gesture and went on with her supper. It wasn't half as nauseating as it looked and fresh air and exercise had made her hungry.

When at length she went to bed her last thoughts before trailing off to sleep were of the tall stranger with the uncultured drawl who had overtaken her amidst the primroses.

Next day the school occupied Evelyn's attention so completely that she had little time to think of anything else, but at the back of her mind she still reserved the belief that she liked North Point far better than Eagle's Bend. The children of the hick town were about on a par with their parents: by no means bright, downright insolent in many cases, and obviously loath to learn. There was another local woman teaching there, and she had seemed only too willing to hand over most of the responsibilities to Evelyn. She had wondered about this to begin with, but towards the end of the day she was beginning to understand why.

The close of school in the late afternoon left Evelyn wondering whether a prison sentence could be much more rigorous.

She arrived at Ma Granson's in time for tea, came into the dining-room from upstairs freshened up and wearing silk shirt and riding breeches in readiness for an evening's walk to clear her mind of the day's cobwebs. Then, as her eyes swept the faces at the table, she gave a start.

The cattleman and his wife were there. Joe Granson was absent; but in his place was a man with broad shoulders, well-brushed dark hair, and a swarthy clean-shaven face.

Overcoming her momentary hesitation Evelyn sat down and shifted uncomfortably as she beheld the big man grinning at her politely across the table.

'This is Mr Jackson,' Ma Granson said amiably, cutting bread vigorously. 'He's only just come to stay here – late this afternoon. He's taken up work in the town. An' Mr Jackson, this is Miss Ward, teacher at our school. . . It's real glad I am to find more boarders in this place o' mine. I was sort of beginnin' to wonder where th' next lot o' money were comin' from. But fer the kindness of Sheriff Padgett I wouldn't be here nohow, I reckon.'

There was silence. Evelyn gave a brief, hard smile. 'Mr *Jackson* and I have met, Mrs Granson,' she said.

Ma Granson looked surprised, then shrugged. 'Well, that saves me a lot of trouble in introductions, eh?'

Jackson looked at her suddenly. 'How'd you mean, Ma – the sheriff's kindness keeps you livin' on here?'

'How'd I mean? He owns this here place, an' th' land it's built on – an' don't you forget it! I pay him rent – or should do; but I ain't paid any in some time, things bein' as bad as they are. He could chuck me out if he wanted – but he doesn't. He gives me a chance to recover – and that's what *I* calls the act of a gen'leman.' Jackson nodded slowly as though thinking about something, then his dark eyes went back to Evelyn as she went on silently with her tea.

'I told you not to go a-jumpin' to conclusions about me, Miss Ward,' he commented drily. 'I don't look so bad now I'm cleaned up, do I?'

'I'm not in the least interested how you look,' Evelyn replied, shrugging. 'Because you happen to have found Ma Granson's is the only rooming-house in the district is no reason for you to make advances to me.'

He looked at her, the scorn in her violet eyes, then with a grin he took the plate Ma Granson handed him.

Thereafter Evelyn maintained an absolute quiet, and the moment she had finished her meal she got up from the table, pushed her chair under it decisively, then strode from the room. Jackson watched her slender figure in the shirt and breeches, the dark hair flowing smoothly about her head then he got up too and hurried after her. He began to catch up as she walked with high-chinned independence down the main street.

'Say, Miss Ward, you're likely to trip over if you keep your chin that high!' His voice behind her only made her elevate her jaw even more – then it happened! Her toe stubbed on a hard-baked wheel-rut and she landed flat on her face in the dust. Hot and angry, she realized she was being raised gently to her feet again. 'Can't say I didn't warn you,' Jackson murmured.

'Why can't you leave me alone?' she flared at him, batting at her soiled shirt and breeches.

. He contemplated her, and the deep humour in his dark eyes only infuriated her the more. She did realize, though, that he didn't look at all like a hobo now. His clothes were clean and he carried a six strapped low on his thigh. He had not had it the evening before, Evelyn remembered, anymore than he'd had the clean check shirt and black pants.

'Look, miss . . .' A grin broke his craggy face to reveal teeth white and strong as a horse's. 'I'm new to this town – same as you told me you were last night, remember? You can't blame a feller for wantin' to sort of team up with you, if only so's we can explore the local scenery.'

'I'll explore the scenery by myself if I want to, and I'll thank you to stop following me around!' Evelyn's violet eyes were still full of anger. 'What would *I* want with a hobo like you trailing with me . . . ?' Her scorn died away somewhat and she looked at him in gathering doubt.

Jackson looked down at her critically. 'You've got me all wrong, Miss Ward. I ain't no hobo – leastways not any more. Since I got me these clothes I've sort of become a gentleman.'

'Even a gun, too,' she added briefly, glancing at it in its holster.

He nodded, and they both began walking as though it were the natural thing to do, moving gradually along the high street towards the open spaces beyond.

'What are you exactly?' Evelyn demanded at length.

'Me? Oh, just a one-time ranch foreman with a habit o' driftin' around. I'm thankin' my stars right now that I happened t' drift here. Don't often see one as purty as you .'

Evelyn gave something resembling a sniff.

'But for you I don't think I'd stick around in a dump like this,' Jackson added, casting a dubious eye at the false fronts and the cowpunchers and women sunning themselves in the evening warmth. 'I'd sooner have North Point.'

'You're from North Point?' Evelyn cried, suddenly enthusiastic.

'Sure am – sort of, leastways. I was there afore I came on here.'

'I'm from there, too! Originally, that is . . .' Evelyn did not know why she went on talking to him: she just did, and that was all there was to it. 'I was born and raised there: my father and brother are still there, in fact. I studied for examinations and things and got myself fixed up with the education authority. They said they had a job for me here – so here I am. But I don't like it,' she finished slowly. 'I'd much rather be an outdoors girl.'

Jackson said nothing. He went on walking easily beside her, apparently turning her statements over in his mind. They had reached a veritable paradise of Mariposa tulips and sweet-pea blossoms before he spoke again.

'Feel like sittin' down, Miss Ward? Just so's we can talk a bit?'

'Well, I . . .' Evelyn hesitated, fascinated by the wonder of the spot into which they had unexpectedly come. It lay two miles beyond Eagle's Bend – a glade at the foot of the all-surrounding mountains.

Cool wind stirred cedars and sycamores; only the sound of a busy little daw could be heard over the eternally whispering leaves.

'I reckon,' Jackson said, fists on his hips as he looked about him, 'this here is the sort o' spot to make you forget people – an' the loco things they do sometimes.'

3

Evelyn seated herself on a low, squat rock and he settled beside her, strong brown hands dangling between his knees.

He gave her a quizzical sideways look.

'You said something strange just now – that you don't like teaching?' he asked finally. 'If you set out to be a schoolma'am, an' got just that, what's wrong with it?'

'Everything!' The girl gave a moody sigh. 'I'd sooner be a ranch-girl – only Dad and my mother wouldn't let me. Said I wasn't cut out for it.' She suddenly made up her mind to confide in this stranger.

'I've a brother – Barry – who's three years older than me. My dad has been grooming him in the ways of the West ever since he was a small boy, able to ride his first pony. He practically runs the ranch now and is set to take over completely when Dad gets too old for it.'

'An' you?' Jackson prompted, deeply interested in the girl's story.

'Mother was determined that I'd receive a different kind of education – the book kind. I'd have loved to have been out riding alongside Barry, learning all the outdoor skills, but my mother would have none of it.' The girl smiled ruefully.

'I guess she meant well . . . and in some ways I'm grateful. When she contracted a fatal illness three years ago, she made me promise that I'd go East to complete my education. Naturally, Dad and Barry agreed with the idea, so I had to keep my promise . . . So here I am. Honestly, though, I'd sooner swing a lariat than teach a pack of kids; I'd sooner rope a steer than mull over history books. I'd like nothing better than to be back home helping to run the Sloping S.'

'But you can't neither shoot nor rope?' Jackson asked with a grin. 'Ever handled a stockwhip?'

'No . . .' Evelyn stared absently into the woodland. 'I can ride a horse and that's about all. Even that was only because Dad's foreman, Clem Hargraves, took pity on me. I – I sort of never found anybody who'd take time teaching me to shoot or rope.' Jackson's grin widened and for a moment the girl thought he was adjusting his gunbelt, then to her surprise she saw he was uncoiling a length of strong, flexible cord from about his waist.

'Just t' keep it handy,' he explained. 'Never can tell. Lookee-here, I'm an outdoors man: you're an indoors girl. I reckon we might get to know each other better if I showed you a few of the tricks.'

'With – the rope?'

'Sure, we can start with the lariat. Why not? I'm no amateur, being an ex-foreman.'

Evelyn hesitated briefly, then she smiled, the first genuine smile she had conferred so far. This hobo, wanderer, cowpuncher, whatever he was, certainly had a way with him. She got to her feet and he did likewise . . .

For some considerable time she was casting the lariat in the woodland clearing, but graceful though her efforts were and patiently though Jackson taught her, she failed within inches each time to lasso an upstanding tree stump a few yards away.

'Never mind,' Jackson said finally, smiling. 'You'll figure it out in time if you'll let me help you a bit each evenin', mebbe. Tomorrow I'll show you how to handle a stock-whip, which every rancher needs to master . . .' He rolled a cigarette slowly as he spoke, lighted it by snapping a match on his thumbnail. Then he shook his head as she handed the rope back to him. 'Keep it. You can practise when I'm not around. It's a good rope, so don't lose it.'

She nodded and began coiling it as she studied him. A frown had drawn her fine eyebrows together.

'I can't quite make you out, Mr Jackson,' she said frankly, at last. 'You don't sound to me as though you should really speak like a trail-hitter. Now and again you even lapse into quite good speech. And there's a definite quality in your voice, too. . . How did it happen you never got yourself educated?'

He contemplated her seriously. 'I dunno. Just never got around to it – but you can teach me the fine points in return for the rope stuff I'm learnin' you, if you like. . . Say!' he broke off suddenly. 'The time sure has flown. . . it's gettin' kind of late. We'd better get back. Don't want people to . . . uhmm . . . think things, do we?' The girl looked at him sharply, then turned away to hide a smile.

Evelyn's next day at the school was no happier than her earlier experience. Somehow she managed to get through the day, and the sound of the bell at the end of the afternoon sounded like sweet music.

By prior arrangement, following their whispered conversation over breakfast at Ma Granson's, they met again at the same spot in the early evening, and Evelyn's 'lessons' continued.

Several hours later, Jackson was silently marvelling to himself at the girl's dexterity with the stockwhip he'd given her, as she managed to snap clean off the flower heads of a bunch of loco weeds at a distance of twenty paces. It seemed Evelyn Ward really was an outdoors girl.

'OK, that's pretty good,' he approved. He made an active movement. 'Now, how's about some gun practice huh? Ever handled a six?'

'Many a time, but I can't seem to get a bead on it.'

He grinned and whipped his iron from the holster. 'Nothin' to it. Watch.'

He fired as fast as he drew, shooting straight from the hip. A distant sapling split in twain. It was not his grand marksmanship that gripped Evelyn's attention, though: it was the gun he was holding. The barrel had a notch across it, just as though a bullet had ricocheted from it some time or other . . .

'Tryin'?' he asked, handing the six to her, butt foremost.

She stared at the gun fascinatedly, then sharply into his brown, square jawed face.

'No. No, I'd rather not . . .' Her mouth hardened. 'Now I *know* that your slang is a pose! You can talk properly when you want – only you don't want, in case it might get you in a spot.'

He looked at her in silent curiosity but said nothing.

'This is going to get you straight into the sheriff's office, *Mr Jackson*!' she went on bitterly. 'You're the masked rider who talked to me in the stagecoach when I arrived here – when the gold was stolen. I recognized that gun again. . . And I thought you were honest, hobo or otherwise.'

He looked at the gun, then back at her. His eyes narrowed.

'Look, Miss Ward, you'd better think things over afore you start spillin' anythin' to Sheriff Padgett . . .'

She turned away impatiently, throwing the stockwhip on to the ground. Jackson slowly holstered the gun. Brooding, he picked up the stockwhip, and put it down the side of his right boot. He watched her until she had disappeared among the sycamore trees. He smoked his cigarette through and meditated, then he tossed down the stub and ground it out under his heel. Moving with sudden decision he headed out of the glade and presently regained Eagle's Bend's main street . . .

Entering the Grey Pearl saloon he gazed across the smoke, rattle of poker chips and clink of glass, his keen eyes searching for one particular face. At last he saw it. Joe Granson was busy playing poker in a far corner. Jackson ambled slowly through the smoke amidst the thump of the tin-pan piano and the stench of stale liquor. Finally he waited until he caught Joe's eye and then jerked his head to him. Joe nodded slowly and got up from the table. He came across the saloon, hand on the butt of his solitary holstered gun.

'What's on your mind, Jackson?' he asked briefly.

'Plenty,' Jackson answered grimly. He moved to a nearby table and they both sat down, ordering whiskey. Then Jackson tightened his lips. 'It's that perishin' school-ma'am,' he explained.

'You mean Evelyn Ward? What about her?'

Jackson swallowed his whiskey and brooded for a moment.

'She's tumbled to somethin' about me I'd sort of hoped she never would. Might get me in bad with th' sheriff, too.'

Joe grinned. 'You been doing something you shouldn't, pardner?'

'Yeah. . . A stick-up. I figured that if I came into town here the thing'd blow over – but it don't look like doin' it now.'

'Where was this stick-up?' Joe asked slowly.

'Never mind!' Jackson's dark eyes glared at him. 'That's my business, ain't it?'

Joe sat back in his chair and lighted a cigarette. 'OK. I just wondered. But what do y'expect me to do? I've helped you a good deal as it is, don't forget. You wandered in here the other night and I fixed you up with clothes from the store, then I told you to board at Ma's place where you'd get the best treatment. Ain't much more I can do.'

'I ain't sayin' as I don't appreciate it, Joe, even if you did take what bit o' money I'd got for the privilege.'

'You should worry! I got that job for you through my influence with the sheriff, didn't I?'

'Yeah, but – Cowpunchin' ain't what I want, Joe!' Jackson made a restless movement and lowered his voice. 'I'm used to livin' dangerously, if you know what I mean – gettin' money the tough way, as long as it's worth gettin'. Up t' now I never got me anythin' much – an' what bit I did get I had to leave afore somebody got wise to what I'd done and started on the prod for me. I'm sorta wonderin' – d'you know anythin' in this here town worth crackin'? I've a hankerin' to be after somethin' big and easy.'

Joe reflected, smoke drifting in his blue eyes.

'I might know of something,' he said finally. 'But I'd have to think it over. S'pose you and me take a little walk tomorrow morning afore we both go to work? We'll have breakfast early.'

'OK,' Jackson agreed. 'But if that Ward dame starts to talk to that sheriff in the meantime, I'm goin' to be hogtied.'

'I don't think she will.' Joe tightened his lips. 'An' even if she does I can fix Sheriff Padgett good and quick. Him and me have an understanding, *sabe*? An' look here, what was there about you that that schoolma'am recognized?'

Jackson considered his empty whiskey glass. 'I'm not figgerin' on tellin' you that, Joe. All I want is easy money – an' quick!'

Evelyn Ward, however, did not go immediately to Sheriff Padgett – not because she had any doubts as to what she had seen, for that six-shooter had definitely been the same one used by the leader of the masked hold-up gang – but because of her inmost feelings. There was something about the tall, raw-boned outdoors man from nowhere that she liked, and liked immensely. She did not believe in such a thing as woman's intuition: in fact she was pretty sure it was something of a misnomer – but she *did* believe in instinct, and for this reason held back.

When she had left Jackson she had been fully resolved to go straight to the sheriff, then somehow. . . Well, now she was in her bedroom, idly casting the rope he had given her the previous day, trying to rope the brass knob on the end of the bed.

There was something somewhere that she could not fit into place in her mind. She smiled faintly as, more by luck than judgement, she landed the noose square over the bedrail knob. She left it there and began to undress, to find her sleep more or less disturbed by worrying dreams. As a healthy-minded young woman she did not credit that she was in love, and yet. . . After all, Jackson – hold-up man or otherwise – was certainly an eyefull for any young woman of twenty-one with aspirations for the future and a hatred of school teaching . . . .

As she dressed the next morning she even realized that she was looking forward excitedly to seeing him again, to perhaps getting an explanation from him – *anything* to prove that she had miscalculated somewhere. She even took down the lariat with her in the hope of asking some questions to open up conversation. Her hopes were completely dashed when she found only Ma Granson and the cattleman and his wife at the table.

'Mornin', Miss Evelyn,' Ma Granson greeted her, smiling. 'You look real bright this mornin'.'

'Do I?' Evelyn smiled faintly and settled in her chair, hanging the coiled lariat over the back of it. 'Must be the spring weather.'

'Must be . . .' Ma Granson eyed her steadily. 'What's the idea of the rope, anyroad?'

'That? Oh – just some tricks I'm practising. To – to show the kids in school. Er – where's Mr Jackson and your son this morning?'

Naturally it didn't matter a hoot where the son was, only it made the enquiry about Jackson sound less blatantly obvious.

'Out,' Ma Granson answered laconically, handing over the breakfast. 'They had a bite early an' then went off somewheres. I wouldn't know. My Joe does a lot on his own account, I reckon, ever since his father died. Sometimes

I'm a-wonderin' what he gets up to!'

Evelyn nodded depressedly and began her meal. It surprised her to find that she had not much appetite for it. Halfway through she abandoned it altogether and picked the lariat from the chair as she got up.

'That all you're havin', Miss Evelyn?' Ma Granson asked in surprise.

'Yes, thanks all the same. I'm not as hungry as I thought.'

Before she could be questioned further she left the room, swinging the rope idly in her hand, and stepped out into the bright morning sunshine. Lost in her own thoughts she followed the main street absently towards the school at the far end of town. Then, gradually, her feet slowed.

'Children!' she whispered. 'A whole day stuck in that stuffy hole trying to teach 'em sense. I can't do it! I've too much else on my mind! There's only one sure cure for the way I feel and that's fresh air and sunlight.'

Her decision to desert complete she turned sharp left and headed towards the town's livery stable. Within a few minutes she had hired out a small pinto and led it back along the main street, the rope Jackson had given her now looped over the saddle horn.

One or two men and women in the street or on the boardwalks paused and looked amusedly at the sight of the girl in her bright summery frock leading the horse – but the one who stared the hardest was undoubtedly Mrs Granson as Evelyn came hurrying into the rooming-house.

'What's wrong, Miss Evelyn?' she asked blankly. 'I se'ed you through the winder. That your horse fastened to the tie-rail out there?'

Evelyn nodded, hurrying towards the stairs. 'I'm not feeling too well, Mrs Granson. I'm going to change and then go for a ride.'

'Well, I'll be gosh durned,' Ma Granson observed, shaking her head – and she waited until Evelyn came hurrying down again in shirt and riding-breeches.

'You sure you can ride that pinto?' Ma Granson asked doubtfully. Evelyn smiled a little.

'Just watch me. That's one thing I *can* do properly!'

The way she vaulted into the saddle was clear proof of that. In fact, with that one action she seemed to change from a girl of education into one of the outdoors. Her knees pressing into the pinto's sides she went off down the main street in a cloud of dust, the wind thrashing back the dark hair from her face. For the first time since she had ridden on her father's ranch near North Point she felt at home again. It rid her mind of the clouds produced by Jackson, of the thought of little girls and boys who must at this very moment be wondering what had become of her. She dismissed the thought. The other teacher at the school could easily cover for her, at least for today.

Careless of where she went she turned right at the end of the street, following the long dusty trail she had traversed in the cramping, rattling confines of the stage. She avoided the actual trail as much as she could, sending the pinto galloping furiously through the endless fields of brittle-bush. Presently the mountains began to loom as she neared the pass where the hold-up had occurred. It brought back unpleasantly sharp memories to her. Then suddenly, something else!

She pulled hard on the horse's reins, slowing him down. For just a moment, from this higher elevation, she had caught sight of two men. They were some distance away on the other side of the trail itself, half hidden amidst rocks and weary-looking cedar trees. There was no doubt that one of the men was Jackson and the other Joe Granson.

The pinto halted. Evelyn stared fixedly, a perfect view being given through a cleft in the rocks beside her. It was not so much the sight of the two men that was unexpected as the heavy black box at their feet, the very one which had been taken from the stage. Judging from the hole in the nearby arroyo it had been dug from there. Immediately the carefree mood went from Evelyn. She was back again with harrowing suspicions, with her grim realizations of what she ought to do. Instinct or no instinct there was *no* doubt about this. She set her lips, turned the pinto's head round, and started off back through the brittle-brush along the way she had come. Neither Jackson nor Joe Granson saw her come or heard her go. They were too far out of earshot. Their horses knew, though, but to their restive shufflings the men paid no attention.

'Well,' Joe said easily, nodding to the box and lighting a cigarette, 'you can't want any better proof than that – you and me talk the same language, Jackson. I couldn't do anythin' last night because I had to ask my two pals, Jed Thompson and Mike Cline, if I ought to trust you. They said if I thought you were shootin' square it was all right with them. You say you want to make easy money? Now you know how you can do it. I don't know what *your* small time racket was, but this is big stuff. There's ten thousand dollars in gold in this box.'

'Yeah . . .' Jackson looked down at it pensively. Then his dark eyes narrowed as he looked at Joe sharply. 'There's one thing I don't get, Joe. What's it a-doin' buried in that arroyo there? Are you waitin' for the heat to go off?'

'That's it. If it comes to that I might as well tell you – I'm waiting for Sheriff Padgett to give the word to bring the box into town – by night of course.'

Jackson stared.

'The sheriff? You gone plumb loco?'

'Nope.' Joe gave a wide grin. 'I told you I had influence with him. I have! Out of this gold my two pals and me get fifty per cent split between us, and Padgett gets the other fifty per cent. I suppose he has his own ways of getting rid of the gold because he pays me off in dollars . . . Whole setup's simple enough. He knows when the gold transfers are made and by which stage. Me and my two boys do the rest. Get it?'

'I get it, yeah . . .' Jackson rubbed his jaw. 'Nice little racket, I reckon. I see now why Padgett didn't go on the prod for the hold-up men. I heard he never stirs his stumps to look for th' robbers. Wouldn't pay him nohow.'

'You said it,' Joe acknowledged calmly. 'And that ain't *all* I get out of it, feller. He's as much in my hands as I'm in his. You know as well as I do that my ma's rooming-house isn't doing as well as it might, an' you know too that Padgett owns the place and the land. Padgett would have kicked her out long ago if I hadn't told him how much I'd say if he did. So he leaves her alone. I've got money, of course, from the last haul – an' I'll have more from this, but that isn't no reason to pay Padgett a rent. 'Sides, I reckon a feller owes his ma that much.'

'Uh-huh,' Jackson agreed, thinking. 'But what do you figger doin' with your money? I don't see you spendin' it freely.'

'I'm too smart for that. I'm collecting all I can and then blowin' town. Seems like I ought to. There's a little matter of a dead man I had to fix during the last hold up. I've gotten away with it up to now, thanks to Padgett – but in case things catch up I want to be on my way. Just let me get my due from this haul, and from the next one – then I'm off.'

There was silence for a moment. Joe threw down the cigarette and stamped on it.

'I wish you could have seen the way Sheriff Padgett led up to asking me to help him,' he said, musing. 'He knows I've got a bit of education and plenty of brains, and he sort of let me know things without involvin' himself. Smart feller, the sheriff; but I'm just as smart, I reckon.'

'And where do I come in?' Jackson demanded. 'I don't get nothin' from this caboodle!'

'You bet your life you don't – nor out of the one before this. But you will from the next, which'll be when Padgett lets me know about it. May be any time now, replacin' this lot here which has been "lost". I can do with a guy like you, willin' to live dangerously and fast on the trigger. For a fancy shooter you're ace high with me. Now I've shown you where we hide the stuff you've got to stall off that Ward dame somehow until we're ready for the next hold-up. Then you can take your cut and hit the trail the same as I intend to do.'

Suddenly Jackson's hand blurred down to his holster and the six-shooter became levelled.

'Get your hands up, Granson,' he ordered briefly. 'You're under arrest.'

4

For a second or two Granson gaped, then he raised his arms slowly.

'Well, if you ain't as crooked as a snake in a cactus patch!'

'Mebbe I am. Fact remains you're gettin' on your horse – right now. I've you, the sheriff, and your two pals to pick up. Oh, in case you want my real name it's not Jackson. It's Clayton – Luke Clayton.'

'You – you the same guy as the *Sheriff* Clayton who cleaned up the Gilbert gang at North Point last year?'

'That's me,' Clayton – Jackson – agreed shortly. 'I had to work my way round to getting the truth out of you. Never mind how I come to be here now. When I arrived here, I didn't know exactly where to start. When I met you in the Grey Pearl the other night I didn't know you were the man I was lookin' for – but you had so much to say I thought I'd let you talk, even into selling me some clothes from that store where you work.'

'Nice stinkin' sort of generosity this is!' Joe shouted. 'I even lent you one of my guns so's you could have protection, and now you turn it on me!'

'That's just the way things are,' Clayton agreed levelly.

'To be an apparent hobo, a man on the run, I didn't want to carry a gun to draw attention to myself at first. I took yours because you offered it – but last night when Miss Ward saw it she recognized something queer on it. I could see that by the way she looked at it. Maybe it's the bullet scar on the barrel. Anyway, when she accused *me* of being one of the hold-up gang I realized it must be *you* she was talking about. So, I had to let you talk – and talk – Now I know . . . .'

Evelyn Ward pulled up the pinto outside the sheriff's office amidst a cloud of dust, swung out of the saddle and hurried up the three wooden steps. Sheriff Padgett, sorting out his desk in readiness for the day's work, looked up at her in surprise as she raced in.

'Mornin',' he greeted briefly.

'There's not a minute to waste, Sheriff.' She was breathing hard with excitement. 'I've got the two men who held up the stage! At least I know where they are. Come on – before they get away.'

She half turned back towards the door then glanced in anxious surprise as Padgett sat contemplating her with puzzled dark eyes.

'Hold your horses, miss,' he said. 'What's all this about? How'd you know what happened on the stage?'

'How do I *know*? I was on it! I saw the bandits take the box of gold and everything!'

Padgett nodded reminiscently. 'Yeah, now you mention it I seem to think I did see you get out of the stage. But what's this about two men? How'd you know they're mixed up with that robbery?'

'Because they've got the gold box out of an old watercourse and are talking about it. For heaven's sake, Sheriff, hurry up! They're only a few miles back down the trail. Now's your chance'! Get your deputies and a posse right away.'

Padgett got to his feet ponderously and scowled thoughtfully.

'Two men?' he repeated. 'Who are they? Do you know 'em?'

'Yes . . .' Evelyn hesitated, then set her chin. 'One of them is Granson, and the other is that man Jackson who's only just got into town.'

'*Jackson!*' Padgett gave a violent start, then he whipped up his two gunbelts and strapped them about him quickly. 'I reckon I don't need a posse for this. I can handle it myself. Let's be going.'

He gave his belt buckles a final slap and followed the girl outside. As she leapt into the pinto's saddle he untied his own horse from the rail and followed her at a swift gallop out of the main street and so, as fast as they could go, back to the spot where she had first seen Jackson and Joe together.

'See?' she asked urgently, nodding through the cleft in the rocks as the sheriff and she drew rein.

Padgett nodded grimly. 'I see all right – a durned sight too well! Somethin' there I don't quite cotton on to. Looks like the bigger feller's got a bead on Joe Granson.'

Evelyn looked intently, with puzzled wonder. There was no doubt of it. Jackson had a six-shooter levelled and Joe Granson had his hands raised.

Silently Padgett slipped from his horse and unholstered his guns. He gave a jerk of his head.

'You'd better be on your way, ma'am. There may be

some fancy shootin' around here an' it's more 'n possible
you might get hit. Start movin'. Get back to town. *Go on!*'

Evelyn nodded and turned the pinto's head, but she
only went a short distance and then dismounted. Silently
she crept among the rocks and at the same time inched
her way down to a spot near the trail where she came
within earshot and yet could remain hidden. Her eyes travelled to Sheriff Padgett some little distance off, his back to
her and moving silently with guns cocked . . .

'I'm not movin' for you or any other durned sheriff!'
Joe was declaring fiercely. 'Only a skunk would use a guy's
own gun on him, anyway.'

Evelyn frowned and then suddenly clapped a hand to
her mouth. Sheriff? Was that just a careless phrase, or did
it mean – *own gun!*' In bits and pieces the puzzle began to
fit into place. She half started to shout and then suddenly
stopped at the explosion of drama in front of her.

Abruptly Joe ducked and dived simultaneously, bringing up his right fist. Jackson – Clayton – dodged instantly
but the six-shooter was whipped from his hand. He hesitated, then whirled at the sound of Padgett's grim voice.

'Okay, feller, make no moves. Stand where you are!'

Slowly Clayton raised his hands. Padgett stood with his
guns levelled, grinning fiercely. Then his eyes flashed to
Joe as, sullen-faced, he thrust his marked gun into his belt.

'Get busy explainin', Joe!' Padgett snapped. 'How
much have you told this guy?'

Joe looked up quickly. 'Told him? Burn me, you saw
he'd got me with my own gun, didn't you? How was I to
know he's a sheriff? I told him everything. I thought he
was with us.'

'Everythin', huh? Including all about me, I s'pose?'

'You can't argue with the wrong end of a shootin' iron!' Joe retorted sourly.

'You're darned right you can't,' Padgett agreed. Then abruptly the silence of the morning was blasted by two shots. Joe Granson stared fixedly for a moment, a look of wonder on his face, then both his hands dropped to the red stain smearing across his chest and he collapsed into the dust.

'That's all the use I've got for a yeller-belly like that,' Padgett explained, raising his eyes to where Clayton stood looking on, his hands still raised.

'You made a mistake there, Padgett,' he said quietly. 'I only had robbery charges against you until you did that. Now you've added murder.'

'Yeah? Try and make it stick without witnesses! In fact,' Padgett added slowly, 'I don't reckon dead men talk at all, do they?'

'I reckon not,' Clayton agreed. His voice was completely unhurried, but his big powerful body was tensed like a steel spring, waiting.

'That bein' so, there's only one way to settle this,' Padgett said drily. 'Finish you and make it look as if you an' Joe here had a fight an' shot each other. So. . .'

'*Look out!*' Evelyn screamed, unable to control herself any longer.

Padgett glanced up, startled for a moment. Clayton too was startled, but his mind was quicker on the uptake. He instantly lunged forward for the guns, but he didn't reach them.

Padgett's knee butted up and took him in the stomach, winding him. As he fell, however, he flung out his arms round the sheriff's legs and brought him crashing to the ground. One gun went spinning but Padgett clung to the remaining one.

Evelyn scrambled down through the opening in the rocks, then she flung herself flat as Padgett's gun exploded at her.

'Get clear!' Clayton yelled hoarsely. 'Run for it!'

She staggered up and another bullet whanged after her in a puff of dust. Then Clayton's fist crashed into Padgett's face and flattened him to the earth for a moment. But only for a moment. Frantically though Clayton strove to prevent it the sheriff heaved up with all his great strength, gun still tight in his grip.

Clayton dived for the gun that had gone spinning, got within an inch of it, then he stopped and twirled round as a bullet whanged by his ear.

'All right, wise guy,' Padgett said curtly. 'If that's the way you want it . . .'

He fired again but the bullet went wide as a chunk of rock, hurled by Evelyn, struck him squarely in the middle of the back. He staggered forward and swung round – then back again.

'I'm not mug enough for that,' he said slowly. 'I'm savin' my bullets for you, wise guy – not for a no-account dame who likes heavin' stones.'

Clayton breathed hard and raised his hands slowly. Then he lowered them again and shrugged.

'OK!' His voice was taut. 'Isn't much use my raising them. What are we waiting for?'

'My hand's a bit shaky after that fight,' Padgett explained calmly, with sadistic pleasure. 'I don't want to miss . . . There!' he levelled the gun and sighted. 'That's better!'

Clayton heard the trigger cock back and looked about him desperately then he gave a start. Evelyn had appeared on top of the nearby rocks, whirling a rope with frantic energy above her head. Like a hurtling snake the rope came flying outwards. The noose yanked round Padgett's wrist simultaneously with his firing. The bullet flew somewhere skywards. Pulled by the mighty yank the girl gave the cord Padgett lost his balance and crashed over backwards.

'What th' hell —' he gasped blankly.

Clayton turned quickly and snatched up the gun near to him.

'All right, Padgett. On your feet,' he ordered.

Very slowly, still unable to fathom what had gone wrong, the sheriff rose up, tugged the cord savagely from his wrist.

'Pick up that box,' Clayton snapped. 'Then go ahead of me.'

Grim-faced, Padgett obeyed. He heaved the box on to his broad shoulder and began to stagger forward. He aimed a malignant glance as the excited, somewhat pale-faced Evelyn jumped down fiom the rock and came hurrying past him.

'I – I did it!' she breathed earnestly. 'I actually did it! And I don't believe I could do it again in a hundred years. I had the rope on my saddle horn, as it happened.'

'Good girl,' Clayton murmured, keeping the gun cocked on the broad back in front of him. 'I hope you're satisfied by now that I'm not a hobo and that I don't really talk slang?'

'Yes – of course I am. What happens now?'

'We go back to town, so that I can telegraph Austin for

a marshal to come and pick up Padgett and two other men – then get help to remove Joe Granson's body and reclaim the gold.'

'And Ma Granson?'

Luke Clayton shrugged. 'We'll have to break the news to her – an' it won't be easy. She's a decent old soul. Anyway, Joe confessed to a murder on his previous robbery, so I suppose he only got what was comin' to him . . . Have to see what I can do towards getting a state subsidy for Ma Granson's rooming-house – Hey you!' he broke off, to Padgett. 'Don't move while I get the horses. If you try, I'll shoot you.'

The sheriff waited, silent, his face working. Clayton gave a grim smile as he took the reins of his own and Joe's horse. Then, his gun trained unwaveringly on Padgett's back, they headed back to Eagle's Bend.

When they reached the outskirts of the town, Clayton insisted that Evelyn should go straight to Ma Granson's and rest up.

'I won't be joinin' you, though. I'm aimin' to spend the night in the sheriff's office – which I'm takin' over until a marshal can get here tomorrow.' He nodded at the scowling Padgett. 'I also want to keep an eye on this jigger whilst I lock him up in one of his own cells.'

'All right, Luke.' Evelyn glanced down at her dust-stained clothes and smiled ruefully. 'I guess I can use a bath, at that. But when can I see you again?'

'Can you meet me in the newspaper office – at say ten o'clock tomorrow morning? The *Eagle's Bend Gazette*? Do you know where it is?'

'I can soon find it. It's run by that Mr James, isn't it? I met him once – why, isn't that him coming now?'

Evidently the strange tableau of the three riders arriving in Eagle Bend's main street had already been noticed. Word had spread rapidly. A bunch of men were hurrying towards them, led by a smiling Fletcher James himself . . . .

The next morning there was a special edition of the town newspaper. Its glaring headlines read:

FIGHTING SCHOOLMA'AM ROUTS A KILLER!
*Courageous girl helps in undercover operation
to bring crooked sheriff to justice*

'Where did Mr James get all this information?' Evelyn Ward asked, lowering the newspaper she had been reading. Her face was flushed with bewildered embarrassment. She looked accusingly at Luke Clayton.

'You told me yesterday you were going to send a telegram to Austin! You came here instead, didn't you?'

'Certainly I came here,' Clayton admitted, smiling. He moved slightly from where he had been standing by the window, and the words *Eagle's Bend Gazette* became visible upon it in reverse in the early morning sunlight as he no longer impeded the view.

'I came here *after* I'd sent the telegram for the marshal in Austin. As for my givin' Mr James the story for his paper – why not? If anyone was entitled to it, he was!'

'Entitled to it?' Evelyn wrinkled her brow.

'Sure he was! Who do you think sent for me to come here undercover in the first place?'

Fletcher James smiled broadly as Evelyn glanced at him in surprise, where he stood by a type rack.

'Don't you remember, Miss Ward, that when you first

arrived on the stage, I told you that I intended calling in another lawman?'

Evelyn smiled ruefully. 'So you did! I didn't think anything of it at the time, and had clean forgotten . . . you said something about not being happy with Sheriff Padgett's handling of the gold robberies.'

'That's right,' James nodded. 'I'd better tell you the whole story . . . Y'see, my sister Margaret is married to a rancher at North Point, Seth Edwards —'

'Of the B-bar-20?' Evelyn asked excitedly. 'His ranch is not far from Dad's . . .' She frowned, remembering. 'When I was a little girl I used to play with their daughter sometimes.'

'My niece.' Fletcher James smiled. 'Small world, ain't it? Anyways, the point is that I hear regularly from Margaret by letter. She'd started mentioning that North Point had appointed a new young sheriff, who was making a name for himself upholding law 'n' order in the town. . . So, I sent a letter to Margaret, detailing my suspicions of Padgett, and asked her to pass it on to Sheriff Clayton here . . .'

'So now you know,' Clayton smiled.

'But why North Point's sheriff? Why didn't you send to Austin for a marshal?' Evelyn asked, still puzzled.

James shrugged. 'Because I had no *proof* of my suspicions. Hardly likely a marshal would have been interested without that. I didn't want to risk the possible delay. I knew my sister to be a mighty persuasive woman.'

'She certainly was!' Clayton laughed. Then his expression changed.

'Well, Mr James, Evelyn, I guess I'll have to be leavin' now. My deputy, young Dave Henson, is covering for me back at North Point. It ain't fair for me to leave him riskin'

himself for any longer than I can help it. I was wonderin',
Mr James, if . . .'

'You can leave it to me, son,' James assured him, anti-
cipating the question. 'I'll attend to the marshal when he
gets here later today. In any case,' he laughed, 'your full
report for him is already printed right here!' He held up
a copy of the newspaper.

Clayton turned to look at the girl, upon whose face had
settled a look of dismay that was almost comical. He
reached out and took the paper from James's hand.
'Perhaps you would like me to give this copy to your father,
Miss Ward? Be no trouble for me to call in at his ranch on
my way back to North Point. I'd be glad to pass on any
messages you might have, too . . .'

'Thank you. But I – I was wondering,' Evelyn said hesi-
tantly. 'Couldn't I go with you? I'd like somebody to go
back with me to North Point. Just in case of hold-ups . . . if
you know what I mean.'

'But what about your teaching job, here? You can't be
givin' it up, surely?' Clayton asked, surprised.

Evelyn shrugged. 'I've not been very successful so far.
The children don't seem to like the idea of the discipline
that's necessary for them to learn anything, and . . .'

Fletcher James laughed, and held up another copy of
the newspaper.

'My dear Miss Ward! What do you imagine your pupils
will think of you after they read this – or have it read to
them? Don't you realize that you're now a heroine to our
local community?'

'That's right,' Clayton said, smiling seriously, and
unconsciously taking the girl's hand as he looked at her
directly.

'Those kids will be lookin' up to you from now on. They'll be real eager to work and learn from you. Are you going to walk away from them now?'

Evelyn bit her lip and flashed him a glance. 'That's not a fair thing to say! You know what I've told you . . . how I love the outdoors life, and have always longed for it. And now that you've taught me the things I've missed out on . . .'

'But you didn't miss out on your own education, did you?' Clayton said quietly. 'Remember how you chided me about my assumed trail-hitter dialect when we first met? Don't you think education for children is just as important as outdoor pursuits?'

Evelyn gave a deep sigh. 'All right. I'll stay – but just for the present school term, or until I feel the children have benefited sufficiently.

'I'm not promising anything beyond that! I see my future back helping Dad and Barry running the Sloping S at North Point . . .'

'That's mighty considerate of you, Miss Ward,' James said. 'You can do an awful lot of good around here, even in a short time.' He smiled faintly. 'I wonder, though, if your ranch is the only reason you'd like to get back to North Point? Er – excuse me,' he broke off suddenly, moving to the doorway. 'I've got my presses to see to next door,' he explained. 'Can't leave 'em for too long unattended . . .'

As the door closed Clayton frowned and looked at the girl.

'Presses? Funny, I can't hear 'em running . . .'

'Sheriff Clayton, you may be a smart lawman, but you can be pretty dense sometimes,' Evelyn admonished softly.

'Mr James just wanted to let you say goodbye to me. . .
properly.'

She smiled archly, and put her arms around his
neck . . .

5

'. . . And that's the whole story, Mr Ward. Your daughter asked me to look in on you when I got back to North Point. She sends her love, and plans to return here when she's free.'

Sheriff Luke Clayton paused, and sipped his drink as neither of his listeners said anything.

Jefferson Ward sat impassively. He was a large, craggy-faced man, hook-nosed, with thick, tufted eyebrows under a shock of white hair. His skin was almost mahogany brown, befitting an outdoors man of the West. His son Barry, seated alongside him at the table in the living-room of the Sloping S ranch-house, was shorter, only slightly less tanned, and was recognizably Evelyn's brother. He had the same dark hair, and firm jaw. He sat scanning the front page of the *Eagle's Bend Gazette* that Clayton had brought, spread on the table in front of them. There was a look of frank incredulity on his handsome face.

Clayton became apprehensive as the silence lengthened. He began to think that maybe Jefferson Ward would be furious with him for having caused his daughter to get caught up with dangerous outlaws, risking her life . . .

'Evelyn and I became kind of good friends,' he said awkwardly. 'I'm hopin' you won't mind if I ride out to Eagle's Bend to see her occasionally?'

'Mind?' Jefferson Ward jerked back his head and roared with laughter. 'Doggone it!' he cried, smacking his palm resoundingly on the table. 'I sure as hell don't!'

Barry Ward looked up from the newspaper and smiled. 'You ain't the first man to notice Sis, Mr Clayton. An' from what I've read here – and already know about you – she couldn't do better.'

'If that don't beat all!' Ward senior was shaking his head. 'My little gal did all that! She made good, eh Barry!'

His son smiled broadly. ' "The Fightin' Schoolma'am!".' Heck, Dad, we never imagined that when she set out East she'd end up a heroine!'

'We never figured her for an outdoors gal either – 'specially her mother, God rest her soul.' Ward senior looked across at Clayton, his face wreathed in smiles.

'We're mighty grateful to you, Sheriff, for bringing us this news of Evelyn. Not,' he added, bethinking himself, 'that it should have been such a surprise. Our family all comes from good pioneering stock . . . which is why I told those damned oil people to get off my land last week —'

'Yeah – an' take their measly cheque with them,' Barry Ward put in.

'Oil people?' Clayton questioned sharply. 'Somethin' happened around here whilst I was away in Eagle's Bend? Them prospectors were only just startin' to look around the district when I left.'

'They told us they'd tested positive for oil on our land,' Barry Ward said. 'An' on some of the surroundin' ranches too – Seth Edwards' B-bar-20 for one.' He shook his head, smiling faintly. 'But Dad sent 'em packin' when they tried to buy us out!'

'Damned right I did!' Ward senior snapped, his eyes glinting. 'I'm a cattleman born an' bred, not a damned mole!' He shook his head, and picked up the newspaper. 'Let's forget them varmints, an' talk some more about Evelyn. . . Barry – another drink for our guest!'

Emerton Martin paced slowly about his office, hands dug deeply into the pockets of his double-breasted jacket. He stopped at last beside the window, pondering, gazing out on the busy life of Austin, the capital of Texas.

'You are sure there is no possibility of a mistake?' he asked abruptly, swinging round to look at the man who was seated beside the desk.

'No possibility whatever, chief.' Deake Collins, mining engineer and chemical analyst to the Martin Oil Combine, had not a shade of doubt in his voice. He was a mahogany-skinned man of medium height with light-blue eyes and a firm mouth. 'You sent men out to North Point to see if there was oil – and there is. I've checked it.'

'But the people of North Point won't sell, eh?' Martin asked.

Deake Collins gave a dry smile. 'As you know, I've never been to North Point myself, but I've gathered enough to know that the inhabitants are a lot of stubborn mules. I don't see that we can blame 'em. They know the land they've got is mebbe worth a fortune in the long run so they're just stickin' to it —'

'I authorized those men working in North Point to offer a good price,' Martin protested. 'And the townspeople, or rather ranchers, wouldn't even listen!'

'If you had something, chief, worth twenty thousand dollars, and somebody offered you one thousand, would you take it?' Collins gave his taut smile.

'There's no comparison at all!' Martin snapped. 'My price was low because I have the drilling, equipment, and labour to fix.'

Collins mused. 'If you saw fit to treble your price you might get some action, but I don't think you will otherwise. Isn't to be expected. When land is just oozing oil you don't take the lowest offer that comes unless you're plain loco.'

Emerton Martin took his cigar from his mouth and twisted it in thick fingers. His hard blue eyes turned presently and fixed Collins steadily.

'Show me again how many areas there are yielding oil,' he said.

Collins got to his feet. Unrolling an area map that had been lying on the desk he weighted down both curling ends, then picked up a pencil and pointed it.

'Altogether, chief, there are four sources – which is a mighty lot in an area so small as that covered by North Point and its immediate surrounding territory. These are the four points . . .'

Martin watched as the pencil touched each spot.

'Ranch property in each case; just as I thought.'

'That's right,' Collins agreed, 'and each ranch-owner knows just what he's got. The biggest ranch is the Sloping S, owned by a tough, hard-bitten jigger called Jefferson Ward. An' his son's as bad. If by some miracle you could ever convince the three other ranch-owners that their property is worth selling – which I don't think you could – you'd never break Jefferson Ward, unless mebbe you decided to kill him.'

Martin pondered for a moment and then snatched open a drawer of his desk. From it he took several foolscap sheets.

'This,' he said, 'is a comprehensive report on the chief citizens in North Point, showing those who might be willing to work for us, and those who must be avoided at all costs. It seems to me that the best bet of all is this Dudley Stroud, North Point's leading lawyer.'

Collins nodded slowly. 'What I've heard of him he's about as treacherous as a side-winder.'

'And he could get together a band of trigger-men to help him – er – enforce his wishes?'

'I should think a man of his type would find it plumb easy.'

'All right.' Emerton Martin gave a grim smile. 'Since these hayseeds won't sell I'll blast 'em into it – including Jefferson Ward! Now listen carefully, Collins. Here's what I want you to arrange with Dudley Stroud, and you'll contact him from Karing's Head, which is about half-way between here and North Point. Since I dare not risk being involved I'm making you my go-between. Now, get this . . . .'

North Point, the small town some fifty miles west of Eagle's Bend, had grown up by degrees. Separated by some hundreds of miles from the fertile oil-bearing regions of Texas, it was primarily the centre of a cattle-rearing community. On all but one side – where the Apache Mountains reared – it was surrounded by arid plains, which made a yearly erosion into the cattle land in the heart of North Point itself. It was a territory that only the most seasoned could stand, and even they found it a merciless struggle in the height of summer.

Despite the fact that they knew oil was present, the stubborn ranchers never even gave a thought to abandoning the rearing, maturing and selling of the cattle by which they – and their fathers before them – lived. They had shown as much when they had rejected offers to sell their land to the Martin Oil Combine . . .

Then the enemy came to North Point – suddenly, unheralded. Jefferson Ward and his son Barry were the first to encounter them, just after they had settled to the evening meal. They were quite alone, still in the dark shirts and riding-pants in which they had done their day's work. The ranch foreman, Clem Hargraves, together with the rest of the boys from the Sloping S outfit, had gone into town for the evening. The first intimation Ward and his son had of the enemy was when the main living-room door flew open and a tall, powerful figure, his clothes dusty from riding, stood facing them. The light of the oil-lamps gleamed on twin .44s.

The old rancher was too astonished to speak for a moment. He just stared, as did his son, but the features of the interloper were covered completely with a kerchief and his black sombrero was pulled well down over his eyes.

'Outside, both of you!' he ordered.

Jefferson Ward got slowly to his feet, a proud, arrogant man.

'Who in tarnation are *you*?' he demanded.

'That doesn't interest you, I reckon.' Plainly the stranger was disguising his voice by pitching it lower than normal. 'I said outside – both of you!'

'We can't argue with a pair of forty-fours,' the younger Ward said quickly. 'All right,' he added, to the stranger, and taking down his black Stetson from the hook by the door he put it on.

Jefferson Ward shook his head obstinately, his blue eyes bright. 'I'm not aimin' to take orders from an outlaw!'

'I'll give you just ten seconds,' the stranger snapped.

Jefferson Ward hesitated, dropped his hands to where normally his guns would have been, but like his son he had removed them, belts included, before sitting down to the meal. Now they were on the sideboard, his son's beside them.

His firm mouth set, Jefferson Ward went with impatient strides to the door, Barry following behind him. When they came on to the porch they both paused in amazement. In the starlight, just below the porch's slightly raised height, was a group of a dozen men on horseback.

The interloper came out on to the perch silently.

'You don't know who we are, Ward, and you never will,' he said. 'But we know *you*, and your son, and that you have a daughter who's out East some place. And we know that you had a chance to sell out this spread of yours, and didn't. That's why we're here.'

'What in thunder do you mean?' Ward demanded, swinging round.

'Just this. You've got one last chance to sign away this ranch property and land. I have the deed with me, and a cheque for the amount originally offered. If you sign the deed you will get the cheque. The deed will be witnessed later.'

'The Martin Oil Combine, I reckon?' Jefferson Ward asked.

'The cheque is signed by Emerton Martin himself,' the gunman agreed. 'An' it isn't a rubber one, either. Take it while you're healthy and you and your son get out of here by sundown tomorrow.'

'You expect me to sign under duress?' Ward snapped. 'I'd report the matter to the sheriff straight away.'

'Try and *prove* it was under duress – if you can! On the one hand you'll have the cheque, and on the other Martin will have the signed conveyance. Think fast!'

'An' if I don't sign?' Ward snapped.

'In that case we'll burn this place down and turn your entire herd of cattle loose in the plains to scatter – and mebbe die. An' we'll take care of both of you, too.'

The old rancher gave a slow, grim chuckle.

'If you think you can hogtie me with a story like that, Mister you're plumb loco,' he said curtly. 'I can look after myself —'

'You can't do anything, Ward,' the gunman interrupted. 'You haven't your guns, and the sheriff's no idea what's taking place.'

'I'm not signing anything,' Ward declared, folding his arms. 'And suppose you tell me what good it would do to burn down my spread and turn the cattle loose?'

'It would make it that the land would become your daughter's property because you and your son won't be around to enjoy it! We would buy the remains of the property from her. Everythin' would be put down to an accidental fire in which you and your son lost your lives and the cattle stampeded in fright. She'd sell – and quick.'

'I reckon,' Barry Ward said slowly, 'that there's only one person who'd know all these legal twists, and that's Dudley Stroud – *You're Stroud!*' he exclaimed, glaring at the gunman. 'I thought no ordinary gunman could talk as educated as you do. An' you've got forty-fours! Only Stroud uses 'em around here! you dirty —'

'You can suspect all you like but you can't prove

anything,' the gunman replied. 'And I'm not waiting much longer either.'

'Do what the blazes you like!' the elder Ward grated – then he dived forward; but the .44s blazed simultaneously. Jefferson Ward stopped half-way in his forward movement, hesitated, and then his knees sagged beneath him and he collapsed on the floor.

'Why, you filthy, murderin' butcher —'

Enraged, Barry hurled himself on the gunman, landed a left and a right to the man's jaw and sent him staggering backwards against the porch rail. He dived again, but a tearing white-hot pain through his arm and chest brought him down, gasping. He collapsed weakly over the body of his father.

He was not dead, though he realized his attackers thought he was, otherwise he would have been fired at again. Through a daze he became aware of the next happenings. The gunman hurried forward down the porch steps and shouted orders to his mounted hench-men. There was an exploding of guns and a lowing of uneasy cattle. Dimly, as he lay gasping and struggling with his pain, Barry could see the cattle being driven into the starlit plain.

By sheer will he forced himself up on one elbow, clutched at the wrist of his father and felt for the pulse. Life had ceased.

'Murderers! Cold-blooded murderers!' Barry lay breathing hard and sweating, malevolence and pain contorting his features.

He sagged, only to be jerked back to consciousness as a blazing torch came whizzing on to the porch. Flames kindled the sun-dried wood and with a crackling spurt gained a hold. Another torch came and landed at the further end of the porch. Then another.

Awareness of the danger gave Barry a transient strength he thought had deserted him. He had either got to move or presently be burned to death. He made a useless effort to shift his father's dead body, then on hands and knees, surrounded by billowing volumes of smoke and with spurting flames making avid leaps towards him, he dragged himself along the length of the porch floor and crawled under the rail at the end.

Breathing hard, he lay for a moment – then essaying another effort he got to his feet and stumbled his way into the stables at the back of the ranch house. The effort in his wounded state was such that he thought he would faint.

He released two horses within the stable, and a third one he saddled, led outside, and fastened it temporarily to the stable door. By the back way he returned into the ranch house and, holding his breath against the smoke, reeled into the living-room. He whipped up his twin gunbelts from the sideboard and went out again, buckling on the belts as he went. He untied the horse once more, crawled up into the saddle and, half-lying on the beast's neck, spurred it forward.

Heedless of where he went he rode into the smoke and out beyond the blazing furnace of the ranch house – into the vast open stretches of the starlit Texas plain.

An hour after he had opened his office the following morning, Dudley Stroud had a visitor – Sheriff Luke Clayton.

'Morning, Clayton. What's the trouble?' Stroud sounded – and looked – completely disarming. He had a round, pink face, ginger hair, and the mildest blue eyes.

'Plenty of trouble, I reckon, judgin' by what went on last night at Jeff Ward's Sloping S.'

'Mmmm, yes, I heard about that. Have a seat, Clayton.'

Clayton pushed up his hat on his forehead and sat down. There was in his young, tanned face as much frankness as in Stroud's there was deceptiveness.

'As I heard it,' Stroud said, 'somebody rode in from some place and for no apparent reason set fire to the Sloping S and stampeded the cattle. I suppose Jeff had to run for it along with his son?'

'I don't think he did,' the sheriff answered. 'It looks as if he was shot dead. The Sloping S foreman, Clem Hargraves, dug me out during the night with the news of a charred body in the ranch house ashes. It wasn't entirely burned. On one hand was a snake ring that identified old man Ward – near as can be. His body's in the coroner's office until the funeral arrangements can be made.'

'Just the one body?' Stroud asked, thinking.

'Far as we can discover. Two bullets were found in the ashes immediately below it, so melted by fire we couldn't make out the calibre, more's the pity, otherwise we might have traced them. It looks,' Clayton went on, narrowing his eyes, 'as if somebody shot Jefferson Ward, then set fire to his spread and stampeded the herd. And it was somebody who knew what was goin' on, too, because they chose a time when the foreman and his boys were takin' a bit of recreation in town.'

Stroud reflected and scratched his round chin. 'What about young Barry? What's happened to him?'

'I dunno. Either he was carried off, escaped, or somethin'.'

Stroud asked grimly: 'How do you know *he* didn't do it?'

'That isn't the answer Stroud.' The sheriff shook his head. 'I've met Barry Ward, and I reckon there isn't a straighter shooter any place. I hanker after the idea he was carried off some place and mebbe killed.'

'Possible,' the lawyer admitted, shrugging; then he looked suddenly questioning, 'So what do you want with me?'

'You handled most of Ward's legal business, so Clem Hargraves tells me, and I'm wonderin' if old man Ward ever made a Will concernin' the disposition of his property.'

'Not with me, he didn't,' Stroud answered. 'Why?'

'Have you forgotten that Ward had a daughter – Evelyn? I happen to know that's she workin' now as a school teacher over in Eagle's Bend.' Clayton's voice was grim. 'Naturally, now this has happened I've got to get in touch with her and tell her what's happened. If her brother doesn't turn up again she'll be the owner of the ranch and the land it stands on, won't she – unless there's a Will somewhere to the contrary? If it was in the ranch we can say goodbye to it right now.'

'I don't think he could have made one,' Stroud answered. 'I did all his legal work, so he'd surely have let the Will go through me? But as you say, without any disposition to the contrary the daughter comes next.'

Clayton took off his hat and perched it on his knee, smoothing back his dark hair. 'Look here, Stroud, how long does her brother have to stop away before he can be assumed to be dead?'

'Unless his body is found he *can't* be assumed dead,' the lawyer answered, straightening at his desk. 'Or, if you can find reasonable proof that he might have been killed, then I can get a court order from Austin granting presumption of death and everything will go to the girl as next of kin.'

The sheriff was silent for a moment, thinking.

'Which isn't much to go on, I reckon,' he said. 'All she'll see is a blackened waste of ranch which she can't inherit until we prove somethin' – and a few cattle saved by the foreman and his boys. Right now they're tryin' to find the rest of 'em.'

'For myself,' Stroud said, sitting down again, 'I don't think young Barry Ward will ever return.'

'Y'don't? How come?'

'Because it isn't reasonable to expect it. I'll gamble that whoever made that attack last night is in the pay of the Oil Combine who offered Ward and the other three ranchers a figure to sell their property, which they refused. And since old man Ward has been killed it's next to a certainty that his son has been too. Because the figure was refused certain elements have taken the law into their own hands, wiped out Ward and his son, and left a charred hulk. Later I'll wager somebody will turn up and offer to buy the land cheap.'

'You may be right, at that,' Clayton mused. 'Old man Ward told me he'd already turned down an approach from the oil combine when I talked to him recently . . . And you think that whoever did last night's dirty work doesn't know there's a daughter to deal with?'

'It's possible, isn't it? She hasn't been in this district for the best part of three years and nobody ever talked over-much about her recently. How *could* outsiders know about her?' Stroud reflected and then added, 'Whoever is aimin' to buy the land will finally realize that she's the one who'll have to do the selling . . .'

'Which she will,' Clayton muttered. 'There'd be no point in her holdin' on to a ruin.'

'She'll sell easily enough – to me.'

Clayton frowned. 'Why to you?'

'Because I'm safer for a buyer than a murderer. If *I* buy that will automatically stop anybody outside the town gettin' the property, and our gun-loose friends, or friend, will know they have had all their work for nothing as well as having the law after them. Once I've got the land in my name I can sell it back to the state and they can use it for oil development.'

'Then I don't see why the gal can't be advised to sell it to the state in any case,' Clayton commented.

'She could, but if I buy and then sell it will be at a profit. I want to make *something* out of the deal.'

'I – reckon so.' Clayton hesitated. He did not say he would not have trusted Stroud across the street, so he added quietly, 'All this can only be taken into account if we prove Barry dead.'

Stroud's face was determined. 'If those men shot and burned old man Ward we can be pretty sure they also finished the son – somewheres. I'm going to act on that assumption and try to satisfy the authorities in Austin that a "presumption of death" certificate should be issued. Then the daughter can inherit everything – and sell.'

Clayton nodded, got to his feet, and put his hat on again.

'All right, Stroud, you do that if you want. In the meantime I'll send Miss Ward a telegram and ask her to come over to North Point. I'd ride out to break the news to her personally, only I have to stay here in case there's more trouble.'

'You're not fightin' a gang of unorganized hoodlums on the rampage; you ought to realize that,' Stroud commented. 'If the Martin Oil Combine is back of this, as it seems to be, you're in for some mighty tough opposition.'

Clayton gave a grave smile. 'I don't scare easy, Stroud.'

With a nod he left the office. Stroud watched him go, then his babyish face hardened slowly. His thoughts ran on.

'So Barry Ward got away, did he? Well, I reckon he couldn't have gotten far, not out on the plain. Unless he came into town here . . . ?' He shook his head. 'Couldn't ha' done. Wounded as he was, somebody would have seen him and I'd have heard of it. I reckon he's dead from his injuries, but not in the way I intended it.'

For several moments Stroud brooded, then he smiled.

'As for the girl, it couldn't be easier. And with that property signed over to me —!'

He turned to survey the district map on the wall. Four sections of it were ringed in red ink. Presently he drew a green line through the circle marking the Sloping S. In his own mind that burned-out wreck and the immensely valuable land on which it stood was already in his name. Just a mere girl to deal with!

After he left Dudley Stroud, Sheriff Clayton rode out again to the remains of the Sloping S, where his two deputies were still searching in the ruins for any trace of a clue which might help them, while out on the plains the mounted figures of the ranch foreman and his men were visible, searching for some of the steers which had still not been recovered.

Clayton rode up to the nearer of his two deputies, Dave Henson, and looked at him questioningly, but the man shook his head.

'I reckon we're goin' to get nothin' out of this, Sheriff,' Dave Henson commented. 'Th' only thing Bill an' me happened on is the hoof-marks of a lot of horses. Must ha' been not one horseman but 'bout a dozen. We ain't a cat in hell's chance of findin' 'em.'

Clayton looked pensively about him upon the ruins.

'Seems like you're right there, Dave – but leastways it's something to know we're fightin' a gang of them.'

'What I can't rightly make out is where young Barry Ward went to,' the deputy muttered. 'There are the marks of a cayuse's hoofs movin' plenty fast from what's left of the stables, but I haven't followed 'em because I've been wonderin' if they belonged to a hoss ridden by Barry Ward or by one of them hoodlums. Come to think on it, it's kind of significant that they go in the opposite direction to the rest of th' tracks round here.'

'They do?' Clayton asked sharply. 'You'd better show me.'

He slid from the saddle and walked his horse beside him as he followed his deputy to a distant hoof-trail leading from the charred remains of the stables and outhouses. In all there were three trails, two of them light; and a heavy one going out towards the expanses of the plain. The other two went to what had been the front of the ranch.

'Get your horse, Dave,' Clayton said briefly. 'We'll follow this heavier one and see where it takes us.'

The deputy nodded and went back to the ruins for his waiting mount. He caught Clayton up and together they slowly followed the hoof-prints, moving further and further into the sun-scorched expanse.

'Well, it certainly isn't just a stray cayuse we're trailing,' Clayton commented, an hour later, 'though there were three tracks back there. I'd say two of them were made by horses on their own, but this one carried a rider.'

'Where did he go, though?' Henson stared into the distance.

They had reached the point now where the pasture land ended and the plains began, a wilderness of dust with a lonely scrub here and there, arroyos twisting through the aridity at intervals, one of them leading back visibly to the Apache Mountains, looming blue and invincible to westward.

The deputy said: 'There's no guy livin' who could survive on this plain without takin' a lot o' precautions beforehand. But,' he swung his arm and pointed, 'he'd have Apache Mountains. Followin' the main arroyo it would be bound t' bring him into the mountains finally, as he'd well know, livin' in this district. Up there he'd find fresh water, an' likely as not a cave in which to hide.'

Clayton nodded. 'We'll see if his trail branches off.'

They spurred their horses onwards again until they came to the biggest of the arroyos. In the soft, sandy ground the horse's hoof-trail turned sharply westwards.

'Looks like you were right,' Clayton commented.

They moved faster now, but as they had both feared from the start, they lost the trail when the arroyo reached the stony ground round the base of the mountains, several miles further on. They drew rein and stared at the towering ramparts climbing peak upon dome into the cloudless sky.

'No use, I reckon,' Clayton sighed. 'Can't follow a trail on this rock. There's just a chance that young Ward got this far and then vanished.'

'That don't make sense to me, boss. Why should he vanish? Be more to th' point if he rode back into town and told us all about it, wouldn't it? As things stand we just don't know what we're tryin' to fight.'

'There's one possible reason why he hasn't come back,' Clayton said.

'Mebbe because he's dead?'

'Yeah,' Clayton agreed; then he cast another look at the crags, passes and canyons. 'Still, I'll get some of the boys to look around and see if they can find anythin'. Let's get back.'

7

In the two days that followed Clayton's sending his message to Evelyn Ward in Eagle's Bend nothing more of interest occurred in North Point. Barry Ward did not return, nor could the men employed by Clayton find any trace of him in the mountains. On the other hand, there were no more onslaughts by the gunmen who had precipitated the Sloping S tragedy.

All things considered, Clayton was in a pretty grim mood when on the afternoon of the second day he received a telegram from Evelyn Ward stating that she would be in North Point later that day, by railroad. Feeling anything but happy at the thought of meeting Evelyn again in the present tragic circumstances, he left his office towards 4.30 and wandered to the railroad station where, at a quarter to five, the train arrived.

Of the scant half-dozen passengers who alighted there was no mistaking Evelyn Ward. She took her suitcase from the porter and then walked slowly along beside the train to the platform exit. Immediately Clayton hurried towards her.

She was dressed in a black crinoline-style dress and

bonnet, her dark hair flowing in waves from beneath it. The mourning clothes made her look ten years older, Clayton thought uncomfortably, as he caught up with her.

'Howdy, Miss Evelyn,' he greeted, taking off his hat and then replacing it. 'I can't say how sorry I was to be the one who had to give you the news about your father . . .'

'Yes, and poor Barry, too.' Evelyn turned to him and smiled wanly, speaking in her quiet, cultivated voice. Her eyes strayed to his star badge. 'I'd much rather have met you again in different circumstances, when you weren't acting in your official capacity.'

'Yeah.' Clayton took her suitcase. 'I've made arrangements for your father's body to be kept in the coroner's office until the funeral.' He hesitated. 'I've taken the liberty of making provisional arrangements for the funeral the day after tomorrow, pending your own wishes after you got here. Your home has been destroyed by fire, of course, so I've booked rooms for you at the Mountain Hotel. I think you'll be comfortable there: it's just down the main street.'

'That was considerate of you,' the girl said, 'but of course I'm not a total stranger in North Point, you know.'

Clayton nodded uncomfortably, but did not speak for a while. He was too busy assessing the girl and cursing the fates that had blighted her life – and his own plans on developing their personal friendship. The memory of her farewell kiss in the newspaper office at Eagle's Bend was still strong. He wanted to take her in his arms and comfort her, but now was definitely not the time. Nor did she appear to want to be comforted in such a way.

He stole a covert glance at her, admiring her composure.

Evelyn Ward was definitely not the weepy type: she was not even of the shy variety that usually flourished around North Point. All the grace and poise of a city-educated woman were hers. Despite her mourning clothes, she seemed even more good-looking than he remembered, with a nose only slightly curved whereas her father's had been hooked. In her mouth and chin there was something of his resolution, but she had taken her beauty from her mother. But Clayton could not help but notice that there was now a light of sadness in her wide violet-blue eyes – which he remembered as sparkling and friendly. They alone gave an indication of her inner feelings.

'I'm really sorry I had such tragic news for you, Miss Evelyn,' he said at last, awkwardly. 'It wasn't easy, givin' it . . .'

'I realize that.' She gave a faint smile. 'Just because this is a sad time, you needn't be formal, you know. You can drop the "Miss", if you like. You don't want me to call you Sheriff do you?'

'I guess not. Luke sounds much better . . . Evelyn.' Clayton looked at her gratefully.

'I want you to tell me *everything* about this horrible business, Luke,' Evelyn's voice took on a note of firmness. 'Just how much have you found out – about poor father and my brother, Barry?'

'Very little, I'm afraid. The whole thing looks to me like organized crime. . . Anyway, when you've freshened up I'd like you to come over to my office. It's right across the street from the hotel. I'll be able to tell you everything and then we can decide what you'll do next.'

'Don't you mean *I* can decide what I'll do next?' she smiled. Clayton glanced at her in surprise.

'Eh? Oh – sure!'

'If you don't mind, I'll make my decisions.'

'Yeah . . .' Clayton rubbed his chin. 'Yeah – sure.'

Feeling by no means sure how he stood in the girl's eyes he did not attempt any further conversation. He carried her suitcase into the lobby of the hotel, took up her reservation, and then left her with her promise that she would see him later.

She kept her word, entering his office at 5.20. Now that she had discarded the bonnet, her wealth of black hair was flowing free. Clayton could not help thinking as she came in that no such vision of loveliness had ever entered the drab office during his short term as sheriff. He got to his feet quickly and dragged forth a chair.

'Glad you could make it, Evelyn.' He smiled at her.

'Thank you, Luke.' She settled down and regarded him in cool composure for a moment whilst he lounged awkwardly against his roll-top desk. Then she went on, 'There's nothing to be gained by trying to spare my feelings, Luke. Just let me have all the details.'

'Okay,' Clayton agreed, and proceeded to tell her everything, embellishing the main points that he had had to withhold in his telegram.

'You think then,' the girl said finally, 'that my father – and probably my brother – were killed by trigger-men agents of the Martin Oil Combine? Just to get the land which my father would not sell?'

'Yes. Stroud, your late father's lawyer, thinks so too.'

'Mr Stroud?' The girl reflected. 'Oh yes, father did mention him in his letters now and again. I must see him afterwards. But tell me, do you really mean that you can't find the least trace of my brother?'

Clayton nodded slowly. 'I'm real sorry to have to admit it, but I can't. Mr Stroud is going to apply for a "presumption of death" order so that the Sloping S land can become your legal property.'

'I see . . . And the men who committed the crime? Haven't you found out anything about them? Who is back of it?'

'There's no doubt who is back of it all, Evelyn – the Martin Oil Combine.' Clayton gave a grim smile. 'The actual gunmen themselves are probably inhabitants of North Point who I meet every day, but I'd never be able to prove it. I can never nail 'em until I get them red-handed – and that won't be so easy, I reckon,' he finished sombrely.

'Since you believe the whole thing is engineered by the oil combine, why don't you tackle *them*?'

'Because it would be a darned sight easier to lift myself by my own spurs! You just don't seem to realize the toughness of the thing we're fighting, Evelyn. The oil combine is headed by a president who is utterly unscrupulous – everybody knows it; but that doesn't make him a durned fool. People can talk, and do, even to sayin' he's back of everythin', but there's no *proof*. Without it I can't act. The risk wouldn't be worth it.' Clayton gave a sigh. 'I represent the law, sure, but I'm tied down by regulations. If it were not for that I'd act as a man would act – with guns in my hands and lead for the wrong answers.'

The girl nodded her dark head slowly.

'In spite of what's happened,' she said at last, 'I think my father was right, even if it did mean his death. Why *should* he sell out his property to a bunch of racketeers? *I* wouldn't!'

'No, Evelyn. You're different from the run of women round here,' Clayton responded feelingly.

'That's because I've spent the last three years of my life – until recently – in the city, making my own way. I left North Point to carry out my mother's wishes that I become a teacher, as you know.'

'When will you be goin' back to Eagle's Bend?'

'I've no idea. In the present circumstances, the school and the education authorities have granted me an indefinite compassionate leave of absence. I shall miss the children there, because I was just getting to know them properly. However, events have dictated that I've returned home sooner than I'd intended. I'm free to stay here as long I wish, and I *shall* stay until I have seen whoever murdered my father safely behind bars. Also I want to be sure what really did happen to my brother.'

Clayton nodded, not quite sure what he ought to say next. Evelyn Ward had extraordinary self-possession . . . Then with a radiant smile she got to her feet.

'You've been most kind to tell me everything, Luke, and I appreciate it,' she said. 'Do you think it would be too late for me to see Mr Stroud before I return to my hotel?'

'I reckon not. He doesn't normally shut his office 'til about six. It's four doors down the street from here.'

'Thanks. I'll see you again before long, I expect.'

'I'll sure look forward to it.' Clayton smiled, shaking hands.

The girl left, and with serene composure walked the short distance along the boardwalk to Dudley Stroud's office, knocked on the door, and entered. Stroud swung round from his desk as she came in and astonishment crossed his deceptively bland face.

'Well, well, Miss Ward!' He got up and shook hands cordially. 'Haven't seen you around North Point in some time.' He looked at her black dress. 'I'm sorry about your father.'

'You're Mr Stroud, of course?' she enquired, ignoring his professed sympathy.

'Sure I am. You've never met me before, but your father mentioned you to me many a time.'

'Oh . . . I see.' The girl contemplated him steadily. 'The sheriff told me he expected I'd find you in.'

'He did, eh? Well, I'm glad you got into town.'

Stroud pulled up a chair for her and then resumed his seat at the desk, sitting so that the pearl-studded butts of his .44s projected from their holsters. Stroud always wore them, chiefly because he was never sure how soon his double-crossing activities would catch up on him.

'I – suppose Clayton gave you the facts?' he asked.

'Yes.' Evelyn nodded soberly. 'All of them.'

'It's a bad business,' Stroud sighed. 'It isn't right for a young, pretty girl like you to have such bad news —'

'What I want to know,' the girl interrupted, 'is what is being done about the land my father owned?'

'I intend to get an order granting "presumption of —"'

'So the sheriff told me. It's ridiculous, and you know it.'

'Ridiculous?' Stroud gave a start. 'How'd you mean?'

'I mean that no court would grant such a certificate without absolute *proof*, and so far there's no proof whatever.'

'As a lawyer, I believe I can manage it,' Stroud said, his brow darkening. 'Then you can take over the property.'

The girl smiled. 'I shall do that in any case.'

'You . . . You what?'

'I shall do that in any case,' the girl repeated clearly. 'You can't stop me. As my father's daughter I'm entitled to do as I please with it even though I do not legally own it. The only case where I would need legal ownership would be if I wanted to sell it. That's right, isn't it?'

'Of course,' Stroud admitted, rather blankly. 'But what on earth do you want with a burned-out hulk like that?'

'It needn't stay burned-out, Mr Stroud. I have a little money of my own. Only the ranch house, barns and stables have been destroyed. I can have them rebuilt – and I understand most of the cattle have now been recovered. In other words,' the girl finished, 'I intend to restore the Sloping S to life. Though I've no doubt my father is dead I have the feeling that my brother may still be alive, and that he may return. If he does, then he is the legal owner.'

Stroud scowled thoughtfully for a moment or two. The girl had thrown all his plans into the utmost confusion.

'Something wrong, Mr Stroud?' Evelyn asked pointedly, as the lawyer remained silent. He started.

'Wrong? Oh, no. I was just thinking. If I were to transfer the ownership to you – which I'm sure I could manage – you might be willing to sell out?'

'To whom?'

'Me. And I in turn would sell it to the state so as to stop those oil racketeers getting at it.'

'I have no more intention of selling, Mr Stroud, than my father had,' the girl replied, still smiling.

'I think you're very foolish,' Stroud snapped impatiently.

'Do you? Why?'

'Well, if gunmen were so ruthless concerning your father and brother, you don't think they will be any the less so with you, do you? You're a woman – far less able to protect yourself than a man. In my view, Miss Ward, you are simply trying to commit suicide by restoring the Sloping S.'

'I'll risk it,' she answered, her mouth setting firmly.

'It's still foolish!' Stroud insisted, even with a touch of desperation; but the girl only seemed to be half listening. Her eyes strayed to the wall-map of the locality and fixed on it. Stroud saw the direction of her gaze and wondered what was passing through her mind. Certainly she gave no indication, for she rose to her feet and held out her hand.

'That being everything, Mr Stroud, I won't take up any more of your time,' she said. 'And thank you. If you want me I'll be at the Mountain Hotel – that is until the Sloping S has been rebuilt.'

With that she went out of the office and left the scowling lawyer watching her through the window.

'Damn the girl!' he muttered. 'Blasted city ideas!'

After she had had a meal and changed into riding-skirt, shirt and half-boots, Evelyn hired a mare from the hotel stable and rode the three miles to the remains of the Sloping S. She found Clem Hargraves, the hard-bitten foreman, busy with his men rounding up the last of the cattle, which, during the day, they had been recovering from the wastes of the plain.

He paused in his work and came to the outside of the double corral-gates as he saw the girl riding up. He touched his hat.

'Evenin', Miss Evelyn,' he greeted with a broad smile.

The girl returned the smile. 'Then you haven't forgotten what I look like since I was last here three years ago, Clem?'

'I reckon not, miss. You ain't changed much in th' time you've been away – 'cept mebbe you're a bit more city-like in your talk an' a mighty sight prettier. But you still ride a cayuse the way I taught you to.' The foreman's strong hands lifted her down from the saddle. 'Aimin' to stay long in North Point?'

'I certainly am!' The girl's mouth set with a firmness that reminded the foreman of her father. 'There was only one purpose behind killing my father and Barry – if Barry *was* killed – and burning down everything, and that was to give me a rubbish-heap to inherit so I'd sell to the first bidder and scurry back East. That's just what I'm not going to do, Clem. I want you and the boys to get the ranch house, barns and stables rebuilt.'

'I like your nerve, Miss Evelyn. Most of the women I know of round here would scat mighty quick if their place got burned down.'

'How much will rebuilding cost, do you think?' the girl asked. The foreman turned and surveyed the blackened waste.

'Not so much, I reckon. Timber ain't dear in these parts.'

'So I thought.' Evelyn leaned on the corral rail and gazed over it. 'How are we fixed in other directions, Clem? For cattle and marketable steers, and so on?'

'Barrin' a hundred head we can't find, which must ha' got lost somewheres on the plain, we've got 'em all back. There's close on eight hundred head o' cattle there, Miss Evelyn, an' at least half of 'em fit to sell.'

'Then sell,' she instructed. 'And start rebuilding the place right away. I'm staying at the Mountain Hotel for the time being, so report to me there when necessary. I'm leaving everything else in your hands because I know I can trust you.'

'You sure can,' Hargraves acknowledged, touching his hat.

'Tell me something, Clem,' the girl went on pensively, 'what sort of a man is Dudley Stroud, the lawyer?'

'Sort of a man?' The foreman squinted into the sunlight pouring down from above the western mountains. 'I figure he's crooked.'

'How – crooked?' Evelyn enquired, pondering.

'Waal, I could name heaps of shady deals that that guy Stroud's bin mixed up in. There's another thing, too: it ain't what you'd call crooked but it ain't straight, neither . . .'

'What's that?'

'He wears forty-four shootin' irons. Ain't natural, I say.' The foreman shook his head. 'Hereabouts the hardware's thirty-eights or forty-fives. Pearl-studded forty-fours is all wrong somewheres.'

'Well, I wouldn't know anything about that,' the girl smiled, 'but I don't trust him any more than you seem to. He's worked out some weird and wonderful schemes to get all this land legally transferred to me, after which he intends to buy it from me and then hand it over – for a price, I assume – to the state, to prevent oil racketeers getting it.'

Clem Hargraves spat lazily over the corral rail and his sharp blue eyes narrowed.

'If that polecat ever gits his hands on this place there's only one person who'll own it – an' that's him! State? With *oil* on th' land?'

'Glad you think as I do,' Evelyn said. She unlatched the

gate and entered the corral. 'I'll look the place over,' she added. 'You won't mind showing me around?'

'Be glad to. Leastways, what there is of it.' He paused, suddenly awkward. 'About your father . . . Sheriff Clayton sort of took charge of things, and —'

'That's all right, Clem. Luke Clayton is a friend of mine. He acted correctly. Dad's funeral will be held in town tomorrow at noon. That's one of the reasons I came out here. I was hoping that you and one or two of the boys might attend.'

'We'll *all* be there, Miss. Only natural that we should want to pay our respects. Your father were a fine man.'

8

At about the same time as Evelyn reached the Sloping S, Stroud set off by railroad for Austin, arriving there towards eleven o'clock after a journey through the most arid land of Texas.

He stayed the night at the Columbus Hotel and first thing the following morning presented himself in the office of Emerton Martin, President of the Oil Combine.

From the look on the big fellow's face he was not at all pleased to see his visitor.

'Look here, Stroud,' he said, getting to his feet and shaking hands perfunctorily. 'I thought I told you never to come here or telegraph, without a mighty good reason? Deake Collins is our go-between.'

'I know – but Deake Collins can't handle this.' The lawyer sat down as Martin motioned to a chair. 'It's about this woman Evelyn Ward, Jefferson Ward's daughter.'

'Well?' Martin raised bushy eyebrows and lighted a cigar. 'What about her? You don't mean you can't handle a girl, surely?'

'No, I don't,' Stroud retorted impatiently, 'but I think the only way to do it is to shoot her dead, same as we did her old man and brother.'

'Shoot her?' Martin gave a start. 'Now wait a minute! Didn't you offer to buy her out? You told me you could fix that when we had our first talk about it here.'

'I know I did, but I'm up against it. For one thing I don't know what's happened to her brother Barry. I know I shot him, but his remains weren't found as his father's were. Only thing I can think of is that he was wounded but managed to get away somehow – somewhere. Just *where* I don't know. He hasn't been seen since. That, naturally, makes it that only legal wrangling can transfer the property to the girl because her brother might still be alive.'

'All right, all right, so you bungled it,' Martin broke in curtly. 'What about the girl? When *are* you buying from her?'

'That's why I'm here,' Stroud answered. 'She won't sell! In fact she's decided to rebuild the ranch house, stables and barns and carry on where her father left off.'

Emerton Martin returned slowly to his desk and sat down.

'You mean to tell me,' he said, emphasizing every word, 'that that young kid has the infinite gall to —'

'Yes!' Stroud interrupted, with a firm nod. 'The Sloping S is on the richest oil-yielding land in North Point; the other three ranches are nothin' by comparison. So what do I do?'

'The little lady thinks she'll play games, does she? All right!' Martin thumped the desk. 'She's taking a risk, and so will we. *Get* her, Stroud – and don't bungle it. But don't do it right away . . . Now let me think.'

Martin got to his feet and began his usual slow perambulation of the office, hands sunk deeply into his trouser-pockets.

'To shoot that girl down in cold blood is obviously something we can't do because of the risk,' he said. 'Besides, after the mess you seem to have made of shooting Barry Ward there's no guarantee you'd do any better in trying to get rid of his sister. And it is also useless to attempt anything at the Sloping S until it's rebuilt. Best thing to do is let her get on with the rebuilding. In the meantime take care of the other three ranches on the list. It's possible that when she sees what happens to them she'll think again and get out – on our terms.'

The lawyer shrugged. 'OK, if that's the way you want it.'

'That's how it's got to be. How about the sheriff? Does he suspect anything yet?'

Stroud gave a grim smile. 'He suspects plenty, I reckon, but he can't prove anythin' – and never will. Unless . . . unless,' he added slowly, 'Barry Ward should turn up one day.'

'Why?' Martin gave him a sharp look. 'What does he know about things?'

'He recognized my voice, or thought he did. Not that that will do him much good without witnesses, but I don't want the sheriff even to suspect me. The men I've got following me are hand picked, from right under the sheriff's nose, but not one of 'em will speak because they daren't. I know somethin' about each one of 'em – somethin' mighty unpleasant – which is one reason why they work for me and say nothin'. Otherwise they'd be in jail.'

The president gave a heavy chuckle. 'All right, Stroud, we'll leave it at that. Remember that all the mistakes you make will bounce back first on you and then on Deake Collins. If you go *on* making mistakes I'll have to take action, for my own sake. Remember that!'

'I'll remember,' Stroud promised, getting to his feet. 'You might also remember my percentage when my cut falls due.'

Upon his return to North Point Dudley Stroud did not make the least effort to go into action and strike again with his band of hired assassins. It seemed to him that his absence from the town and his return by railroad might provide a lead for the watchful Sheriff Clayton and – if more trouble happened – set him making enquiries.

When he learned that the funeral of Jefferson Ward was in progress, he decided he had better follow the procession, for the sake of appearances.

It seemed that most of the town was assembled round the graveside. Ward had been a pretty respected man in the district.

Whilst he listened to the short funeral service, Luke Clayton glanced about him. He noticed with satisfaction that Clem Hargraves and the boys of the Sloping S were present, their heads bare as they held their hats. He frowned slightly as he noticed Dudley Stroud in the background, then it occurred to him that nearly all the prominent citizens in the town were present. Nothing unusual in that, considering Ward's standing in the community.

Then, as the coffin was lowered into the earth, Clayton felt a slight pressure on his hand. He opened his fingers and held Evelyn's cold hand as she held it out to him. He swore silently that he would help this brave girl to bring her father's killers to justice.

It was just as well for him that Stroud could not read Clayton's thoughts, as he became one of the first to slip away through the gate to the graveyard at the back of the small church. Instead his thoughts were devoted entirely to his own scheming. All things considered, this was no time to attack the second ranch standing over oil.

In due course, through the medium of the many men he had working for him, Dudley Stroud got wind of activities at the Sloping S. The outfit there, it appeared, was working night and day in shifts on the rebuilding of the ranch house, barns and outhouses. In ten days Stroud heard that the girl had forsaken her hotel rooms and moved over to the ranch, where – presumably – she intended to remain indefinitely. The ten days became fourteen. At the Sloping S the barns and stables were completed. The girl had selected a mount for herself from amongst those used by the men – a speedy pinto – and if her visits to the general store in town were any guide she had by now equipped the ranch house with every needful thing.

Ultimately, Stroud was satisfied that the time was ripe for Seth Edwards and his family at the B-bar-20 to receive a visitation, and so he sent forth the word.

As usual the attackers came by night, about an hour after Seth Edwards, his wife and grown-up son and daughter had finished their evening meal. All of them were in the big, comfortable living-room of the ranch house when the floor-to-ceiling window which fronted the western porch smashed inwards in a shower of glass.

Stroud, his neckerchief up to his eyes and his hat pulled well down, stood there. Dusty riding-pants, a black shirt, and half-boots completed his attire.

'Evenin', Edwards,' he greeted briefly, levelling his .44s.

The tall rancher got to his feet and so did his son. Mrs Edwards and the daughter remained where they were, too astonished to move.

'It's the same thing as happened to Jeff Ward over at the Sloping S spread!' the son exclaimed abruptly. 'We ought —'

'You shut up!' Stroud ordered. 'My business is with your old man. Edwards, you were given the chance to sign away this property a few weeks back, an' you refused. If you don't want the same thing to happen to you as happened to Jefferson Ward and his son you'd better think again. I've a deed and a cheque with me. The deed only needs your signature, assigning all rights to the Martin Oil Combine.'

'You think I'd be such a doggone fool as to sign for a thievin' price like that?' Seth Edwards snapped.

'Better than losin' your life, isn't it?' Stroud retorted.

'I'm not signin' anything!' Seth Edwards declared stubbornly.

'But Seth —!' His wife looked at him anxiously. 'You know what happened to Jeff Ward!'

'An' it'll happen to all of you,' Stroud warned.

'Even supposin' I did sign the deed an' took your stinkin' cheque,' Edwards said bitterly, 'ain't you got the sense to see it wouldn't be legal? It's *makin'* me do it!'

'Under duress, you mean? Ward said that, until I put him wise. You can never prove anythin' when you've got the cheque in your hands and the oil combine's got your signature on a transfer.'

'He's right, Pa,' the daughter said urgently.

'I ain't so sure,' her father argued. 'I've a mighty strong feeling that something *could* be proved . . .'

'One way to find out,' Stroud told him. 'Sign – and then figure out what you'll do next.'

Plain obstinacy settled on the rancher's grim face. 'No thievin' owlhooter is a-goin' to make *me* sign!'

Stroud shrugged. 'OK. Outside, the lot of you!'

The motioning of his guns was sufficient to set the two men and two women moving, and they stepped out on to the porch. In silent dismay the four looked at the dozen or so men in the dim light perched on their horses just beyond the porch.

'Well?' Seth Edwards demanded arrogantly, turning. 'What are you waitin' fur? Shootin' down two defenceless women and a couple of unarmed men shouldn't be too tough.'

'There isn't goin' to be any shootin',' Stroud told him curtly. 'This spread is too near town: sound might carry. I'm thinkin' we can do all we need with four lariats.'

'You mean you'd hang us?' the younger Edwards gasped, horrified.

'All of you,' Stroud affirmed. He raised his voice and called to the men below. 'Four ropes, quick! And this isn't bluff, Edwards,' he added, 'as you'll mighty soon find . . .'

Stroud stopped speaking. Something hard was prodding in the small of his back. A merciless voice breathed in his ear.

'Cancel that order for ropes and send your men away. If they don't go you're finished – and you can tell 'em so.'

Complete bewilderment overcame Stroud. He could see the four members of the Edwards family facing him at the end of the porch, and he knew there were no others about the ranch because he and his men had made sure of that beforehand. Yet now . . .

The Edwards family could see the newcomer in the reflection from the oil-lamps in the room beyond. He was medium-sized and broad-shouldered, dressed in black pants and shirt, while a black kerchief had been made into a hood-bag and covered the face entirely except for the eyes, peering from beneath a black sombrero.

'Do as I tell you!' the voice snapped. 'Drop your guns!'

Stroud let them fall with a clatter, and below the porch steps the assembled men stared in amazement, the intruder's figure being hidden behind Stroud. They began to jerk out their guns and the starlight reflected from the polished barrels.

'Better tell 'em to take it easy down there,' the voice warned.

'Wait!' the lawyer shouted to his men. 'Don't fire! If you do I'm finished.'

'Tell 'em to get going and take your horse with 'em. You're not likely to be needin' it – ever.'

Perforce Stroud had to obey orders. 'Get moving, the lot of you!' he implored. 'And take my horse with you.'

He waited tensely, the gun on his spine never wavering. There was an uneasy movement amongst the assembled men as they whispered to each other. Stroud wondered desperately what they would do. If they obeyed, they had the chance to disperse and escape the attentions of the stranger, and they could also fight again another day. If they did not obey they might, with their superior numbers, overwhelm the stranger – and lose their leader. Then, with a sigh of relief, Stroud saw them turn and set their mounts galloping into the night.

'OK,' the stranger said briefly, glancing towards the group at the end of the porch. 'You folk get back inside and keep yourselves armed in future.'

'Can't we at least thank you?' Mrs Edwards asked.

'Never mind that. Remember to lock your back door next time. I came in that way.'

The quartet moved. The gun prodded Stroud again.

'You start movin' too. Down the steps.'

Stroud had to obey and the stranger followed him, only pausing long enough to pick up the two .44s that Stroud had dropped and push them into his belt. Still with the gun jabbing him, the lawyer had to go round to the back of the ranch house, where a single horse stood tethered to a tree.

'Turn around!' the voice snapped.

Stroud did so and looked at the masked figure intently.

'I'm here for only one reason, Stroud,' the stranger went on, stripping away the lawyer's kerchief so his face became faintly visible. 'That reason is to kill you and afterwards to blast that bunch o' murderers who follow you around.'

Stroud did not lose his nerve, chiefly because it would have been a fatal thing to do at that moment.

'You're not foolin' me, you know,' he muttered. 'You're Barry Ward. Somehow you must have escaped after I shot you.'

'You can think what you like; I'm not admitting anything. Before I'm finished I'll have only one name around this territory, and that'll be "The Avenging Ranger"! The party's over for you, Stroud. Finally I'll get around to the brains behind it all – the oil combine. I don't think I'm far wrong in thinkin' it's Emerton Martin in person.'

'It'll take more than one man wearing a hood-mask to upset the plans of the oil combine,' Stroud answered.

'You think so, huh? You had your chance to kill me, Stroud, and muffed it. Yeah, I'm Barry Ward all right. This time it's my turn and I shan't make the mistake you did.

Nobody knows better'n me that this is plain murder – but you don't think of it as murder when you blast the head off a rattler.'

Stroud shrugged and relaxed but only for a split second; then he lashed out with his right hand and snatched one of his own guns projecting butt-foremost from Barry's belt. At the same instant he drove up his left fist and took Barry under the jaw.

Before Barry could pick himself up Stroud fired, but in his over-anxiety he missed. Barry was on his feet again instantly but he was prevented from aiming his gun by Stroud bringing the butt of his .44 down savagely. Barry flattened out on the ground again, half senseless. Dazed, unable to move for a moment, he fired his gun mechanically. Stroud, though, had dived for the horse tethered to the tree. Even as he vaulted into the saddle he fired again and dust flashed up in front of Barry's eyes.

Clamping a hand to the back of his neck Barry fought his way to his knees, swayed giddily, and eventually managed to stand up. Seth Edwards and his son came hurrying out of the ranch to him.

'What happened?' Seth Edwards demanded. 'Who shot who?'

'You hurt?' asked the son quickly.

'Get – get me a horse,' Barry muttered, breathing heavily. 'That low-down skunk took mine. I've a ride to make.'

'I reckon we'll *give* you a horse, stranger, for what you've done for us,' Edwards said. 'But if you're hurt —'

'No, no, it's nothing. Just give me a horse.'

The son hurried off in the direction of the stables and with an effort Barry steadied himself.

'That guy with the gun was Dudley Stroud, wasn't it?'

Edwards demanded. 'I could tell his voice, even if he were disguisin' it, since there ain't no man else who could be so legal, I reckon.'

Barry did not answer and the rancher added a question.

'Who are *you*, anyway? Only one I can think of is Jeff Ward's boy. Lot o' talk of him disappearing . . .'

'Call me the Avenging Ranger,' Barry suggested briefly, then he glanced up as the younger Edwards returned with a chestnut mare. Barry climbed up into the saddle and without another word dug his spurs into the animal's sides and raced off into the night.

Seth Edwards glanced at his son.

'Who do you reckon he is, Pop?' the younger Edwards asked.

'I asked him, son, but he wouldn't tell me. Mebbe it's a wild guess, but I'd say Barry Ward. 'Bout his size and figure.'

Evelyn Ward was busy at the table beside the reading lamp, going through papers in connection with the restored ranch when a thunderous hammering on the outer door made her glance up in surprise. She looked at her watch, frowned as she saw it was close on midnight; then picking up the .38 which Clem Hargraves had loaned her, she rose and went across the room, taking the oil-lamp with her.

She unlatched the door but left the chain on and spoke through the narrow aperture.

'Well, who is it? What do you want?'

'Let me in, Sis. It's me – Barry.'

'*Barry?*' the girl gasped back, incredulous.

'Cross my heart, Sis. Be quick! I don't want to be seen.'

The girl slipped off the chain and opened the door wide. Her gun came up sharply at the sight of the black-suited, masked figure – then she laid the weapon aside and laughed in tearful relief as Barry pulled off his hat and hood-mask and embraced her.

'Barry!' she whispered, hugging him. 'Oh, thank heaven! you're still alive. Somehow I knew you must be . . .'

Arms about each other they moved into the centre of the living-room. The girl put the lamp down on the table and Barry threw himself into a chair. He gave a slow, grim smile.

'I've never been very far away,' he explained. 'Each night I've ridden down from the hills and taken a look at things. By day I've watched from the hills. Been a long time since I've seen you, Sis. You hardly look like the same girl to me. In fact, you're not! That newspaper story . . .'

She looked at him seriously. 'Let's not talk about me: it's you I'm wondering about. What happened on the night those desperadoes killed Dad?'

'They shot him, as you know; but the bullet aimed for my heart missed. It didn't even lodge in my body and all I got was a chest and arm rip and a good deal of lost blood. I rode out to the mountains and patched myself up with water from a stream, part of my shirt, and a good supply of sleep. I was half-conscious in a cave for a long time, then I realized I was fast recovering and needed food. During that time Sheriff Clayton and his boys came and did a bit of exploring. They even came in to the very cave where I was hiding, but it happens to be a double one with a high wall of rock at the back. I was behind that, with my horse, and wasn't discovered. By night I rode back here, and as I'd hoped, several of the canned foods that had been in the kitchen were in the ashes unharmed, except for the tins being blistered on the outside and the food inside half-cooked. I took enough to last me and my horse a month.'

'But – Barry!' The girl looked at him blankly. 'Why on earth did you do that? Why didn't you go straight to Sheriff Clayton and tell him what had happened – or else get in touch with me?'

'I didn't go to the sheriff because I know – and you know too – that without proof and witnesses he can't do a thing. There's only one way to beat the hoodlums who are dead set on murdering and pillaging innocent ranchers in this territory, and that's to take the law into one's own hands. That's what I'm doing.'

'But that makes you an outlaw!'

'I prefer to call myself an avenger, Sis – the Avenging Ranger. The Martin Oil Combine's back of things. You know that?'

'I gathered as much.'

'The head man in these raids, and the man who shot Dad and tried to shoot me, is Dudley Stroud the lawyer – and here's proof of it. This is one of his guns . . .' Barry tugged it from his belt. 'A forty-four. He managed to snatch back the twin to it. I'm stickin' to this one: may come in handy.'

'Yes,' Evelyn said slowly, looking at it. 'That's his all right. I remember noticing the pearl-handled butts on the day I talked to him in his office, and Clem Hargraves told me that Stroud always uses forty-fours . . . As for Stroud being at the back of things, that's no surprise either. There's a map on his office wall with four ranch areas marked on it, and the only one with a cancelling green cross through it is ours – before I rebuilt.'

'We could tell the sheriff that Stroud's our man,' Barry said, 'but could we prove it? Like hell! Just as we can never prove that the brains behind it all is Emerton Martin. That's why I figured that the best way to act is to become such a source of trouble to Stroud an' his gunmen that they just daren't act. Keep 'em constantly on the jump. It worked tonight – partly anyway.'

'You mean there's been another raid?' the girl asked.

'Sure has. At the B-bar-20; Seth Edwards' place. There's oil under his spread as there is under ours. You see, Sis, there are four ranches in this territory which these hoodlums have to get. There's this one, the B-bar-20, the Sleepy V and the Falling H. Obviously they'll be the ones you saw marked on that map in Stroud's office. It's a big help the oil being limited to those four places. It means the raiders aren't likely to attack anyplace else. The oil yields are on those particular spots and they'll go all out to get 'em.

'Fortunately none of 'em are more than a few miles from each other so it's easy to keep some kind of watch on 'em. That's what I've been doin' – yes, including ours in case they had a smack at you. Tonight I was rewarded. I saw 'em headin' for the B-bar-20 so I went after 'em and got there just in time to save Seth Edwards and his family from a necktie party.'

'And Stroud?' the girl asked.

Barry tightened his lips. 'He got away – but not before I'd made his men disperse, an' if they try again Edwards'll be fightin' mad and ready for 'em, so I don't think they will. If they try anything it will be on the Sleepy V or the Falling H. Else here. But not with me around! It's a pity about Stroud. He took me by surprise, just when I was all set to shoot him.'

'I'm glad you were prevented,' Evelyn said quietly.

'*Glad?* You crazy, Sis? After he murdered Dad?'

'The right answer, Barry, is to take him to Sheriff Clayton.'

'With no proof it would be utterly useless.'

'Then wait until you get some.'

'And how long do you imagine that would take? Men of

Stroud's calibre, smart lawyers, don't go about leaving proof of their actions. I'd never get it, 'cept by accident.'

'For heaven's sake, Barry, don't make yourself as bad as the men you're following!'

Barry looked at his sister pensively, his smile whimsical. 'You've lived so long in Austin, Sis, you've changed your outlook. When I said you were hardly the same girl I meant more than I realized . . . I'm rememberin' what Dad used to say – that a good shooting iron's worth a desert full of words. He was right.'

Evelyn sighed. 'All right, have it your own way. What do you propose to do next, then?'

'Go on as I have been doin'. I'm staying up in the mountains and keeping watch so that I can bust up the next raid when it's attempted. But I need help – mainly in the matter of food. You don't have to keep your movements secret as I do: nothing to stop you riding out with food for me each day, is there?

'Nothing at all,' the girl agreed. 'In fact I'll gladly do it, even though I do wish you'd see the thing sensibly.'

'I've got my own methods, Sis, and I'm stickin' to them.' Barry grasped her shoulders and kissed her encouragingly. 'All right, then, bring me some food along tomorrow morning. I'll be waiting for you at the far end of the central arroyo – remember it?'

'The big middle one which links up with the foothills? Yes, I remember it.'

'OK. Then we can go up to my cave and mebbe chat for a while. Oh, you'd better rustle up some food for my mare, too. Roots and the stuff I can give her don't amount to much. Pity is Stroud's got my horse and this chestnut mare isn't a patch on him.'

The girl watched him as he slipped the hood-mask back into place and then put on his hat.

'I still think you're on the wrong tack,' she said as she went with him to the porch. In the shadowy night Barry paused and looked about him.

'How about Clem and the boys?'

'In the bunkhouse.' The girl nodded to the more distant reaches of the corral. 'One or other of them is always on hand after what happened. I insist on it.'

'Matter of fact,' Barry said, 'I don't place much store on the boys having an eye to your safety. Not that I distrust 'em – couldn't be a squarer bunch any place – but trying to keep always on the watch gets tiring, as I've good reason to know. Besides, they've got to sleep sometime, and when they do they'll do it properly. So the best thing you can do is lock your door each night – as well as the other doors.'

He went down the steps in the starlight and to his tethered mare. Swinging into the saddle he waved once, and then headed in swift and almost soundless speed towards the distant arroyo that he knew by heart. The girl turned back into the ranch house, and in so doing was just too late to notice a second horseman speeding out of the night in pursuit of Barry.

Barry, for his part, soon became aware of being followed. He twisted round in his saddle and frowned into the starlight behind him. The horseman was rapidly overtaking him. Barry dropped his hand to his holster and whipped out his gun. Behind him a revolver suddenly exploded – once, twice, three times.

Dudley Stroud was at work in his office the following morning when the door opened to admit a puncher, just one of the many who made up the male community of North Point, and for that reason unlikely to attract anybody's notice.

'Well, what do you want?' Stroud demanded coldly. The puncher leaned indolently against the roll-top desk.

'I reckoned I'd better check up on you, boss, after last night. Things wus all set for you to be rubbed out.'

'Well I wasn't rubbed out. I'm still here – and I don't like *you* coming here either!'

'Sure, but I got around to thinkin' that I might have to wait a long time for orders. So I came to make sure. What happened? How'd you get away from that perishin' stranger?'

'By using my brains, of course. You don't think one man with a momentary advantage is going to upset our plans, do you?'

Stroud put down his pen and reflected. 'In case it interests you, Hank, our interfering friend was Barry Ward.'

'*Ward*! Did he admit it?'

'Uh-huh – finally. He called himself "The Avenging Ranger".'

'Then he wasn't shot when we raided the Sloping S?'

'He was shot all right, but I must have missed my aim somehow. Last night after I'd escaped I made up my mind to make doubly sure of his identity by asking his sister – at the point of my gun; only I didn't need to because I saw him ride to the Sloping S and then leave shortly afterwards. He won't trouble us again.'

'You took care of him, huh?' the puncher asked.

'Three slugs. He could have made things mighty awkward for us. He went right on ridin' but I know those slugs couldn't have missed. I didn't follow to find out because I was worried the shots might have been heard at the Sloping S, so I got out quick.'

'Mmmm. You *thought* you'd got him at the Sloping S earlier.'

Stroud glared. 'I tell you I *got* him this time – an' if it wasn't so risky I'd ride out and take a look.'

'Just as you say,' Hank responded, placatingly. 'What's next, then? Do we try the B-bar-20 again?'

'Not for a long time. Things have got to have a chance to cool off. The next one we tackle will be the Sleepy V, and that won't be for a night or two. I'll tip you off when. Now get out before anybody comes.'

The puncher nodded and turned to the door just as it opened to admit Sheriff Clayton. His bronzed face was unusually set. He gave a nod to the puncher, looked at him curiously, and then closed the door. He walked over to the desk.

'Mornin', Sheriff,' Stroud greeted casually.

'I'm in no mood for pleasantries, Stroud,' Clayton answered. Whipping up a chair he reversed it and sat down so that his forearms leaned on the back. 'I've had Seth Edwards of the B-bar-20 over at my office this morning,' he continued. 'Lodgin' a complaint against you. He says you attacked him last night with a bunch of hoodlums, tried to make him sign away his property, and threatened him and his family with hanging if he didn't. Same sort of thing as happened to Jeff Ward. What've you got to say for yourself?'

'What do you think?' Stroud asked contemptuously.

'In my business I'm not entitled to think – only to prove.'

Stroud laughed shortly. 'Prove! What would I want

gangin' up on a rancher with a bunch of trigger-men? Talk sense, man!'

'That's what I'm aimin' to do. But I can't help rememberin' you telling me how nicely you've doped it out to get the Sloping S land legally in your name, if Miss Ward hadn't decided to take it over herself.'

'You've sure got a mighty powerful imagination, Clayton. If you're accusing me –'

'I'm not accusin' you of anything because I'm not that loco. Edwards also told me that the only thing which saved him and his family from being strung up accordin' to plan was the arrival of a masked stranger. Edwards thinks it might have been young Barry Ward. What d'you know about that?'

Stroud shrugged. 'Nothing. If anybody has information it'll be Evelyn Ward, I'd say. As for Seth Edwards, he must have gone crazy! I don't doubt that he was probably attacked – same as Jeff Ward was – but as for thinkin' it was *me* at the back of it . . .! What gave him such a notion anyway?'

'He says nobody but a legal man could have known the legal side as well as the man who attacked him.'

'If that's the best proof you've got you'd better start handin' in your badge, Sheriff,' Stroud commented.

Clayton smiled. 'The only thing I aim to do is hand in the murderer of Jeff Ward, and the would-be murderer of Seth Edwards and his family.'

'All right – but the least you can do is have sense enough not to go around accusing me!'

'Don't start anythin' you can't finish, Stroud,' Clayton said quietly, rising; then with a nod he left the office.

His expression thoughtful he untied the horse's reins

from the tierack and vaulted into the saddle, turning the head of his mount so that he left town at a leisurely trot and then went along the trail which, three miles further on, passed the Sloping S.

He was heading for the main gate of the ranch when an approaching rider some distance away across the pasture land caught his attention. Drawing rein, he leaned on the saddle horn and waited, shading his eyes from the blaze of the morning sun. His first guess that the rider was a woman became gradually verified, as presently Evelyn Ward came within seeing distance, dressed in riding-skirt and shirt, her black hair flowing in the breeze.

She seemed to catch sight of him suddenly, until which moment she had plainly been lost in thought. Clayton frowned a little to himself.

'Morning, Evelyn,' he greeted her, as she came riding up. 'Exercise?'

'Er – yes. Exercise.' The smile she gave struck him as unconvincing. 'And I didn't expect to find you waiting for me. Is there anything wrong?'

'I dunno whether you'd call it that or not.' Clayton took off his hat and reflected, studying the girl's face. 'I'd like a few words with you.'

She nodded. 'By all means. Come into the house.'

Clayton followed her horse through the main gateway. When they had entered the cool, shady living-room the girl nodded to a chair.

'Have a seat, Luke, and tell me all about it.' She settled herself against the arm of the chair opposite him.

'The B-bar-20, Seth Edwards' spread, was raided last night,' he said.

'It was? Anybody killed?'

'A stranger intervened – a man in a black hood-mask and obviously an enemy of the outlaws.' Clayton looked at his hands absently. 'Old man Edwards has the notion it could have been your brother come back.'

'Barry!' the girl exclaimed, with a puzzled look. 'But that isn't even possible, is it?'

'I'm asking *you*, Evelyn. *Is* it possible? As his only relative you'd be the first person your brother would contact.'

'Yes, of course,' the girl admitted; then she added flatly, 'But I haven't seen him. Supposing it were him, what would you want with him? He didn't kill anybody, did he?'

'I reckon not, but it's because he might do unless he's stopped that I want a few words with him. From what I can make out it seems pretty plain that he's aiming to wipe out these bandits single-handed. That's a plumb crazy notion, Evelyn. Killin' a man is still murder, even if you kill a murderer. That's why I want to know who this man was.'

The girl was silent, musing. Clayton watched her expectantly. Then as she said nothing he went on talking.

'Y'see, Evelyn, if it wasn't your brother, I just don't know *who* it could have been, because up to last night nobody but your father and brother had suffered at the hands of these hoodlums; so you can see how it looks to my way of thinkin'.'

'Yes, of course I can,' the girl assented. 'But I don't see how I can help you. As far as I know he's dead.'

'Well, OK,' Clayton agreed slowly. 'If he does turn up let me know right away. He's got nothing to fear – at the moment.'

The girl began to wander aimlessly about the room, thinking.

'Hasn't Edwards got some idea as to who the man was who attacked him?' she asked finally.

Clayton gave a cynical smile. 'It was Dudley Stroud.'

Though the girl had expected this she simulated surprise.

'The lawyer? But surely —'

'As sheriff, Evelyn, I'm not supposed to hand out names of people suspected of a crime – but in this case I'm side-steppin' the law and telling you, chiefly because you've lost so much through this banditry, and because I know you'll help me all you can if I tell you all I know. Stroud's back of everything; and back of him is the Martin Oil Combine. I had a talk with Stroud this mornin' and though he denies everything he isn't foolin' me. I'm pretty sure I saw one of the men who works for him leavin' his office this mornin'.'

'But for the moment he's surrounded with legal defences?'

'Yeah. He knows I can't do anythin' without proof.'

The girl walked slowly back to the centre of the room.

'I suppose if you could ever get these men all in a bunch you'd be able to prove all you want?'

'That'd suit me fine,' Clayton agreed. 'With the whole gang in a bunch they'd betray each other just to make things softer for themselves. Separately they'd never do it. At least that's the way I figure it. Come to think of it, getting them in a bunch isn't half as important as getting them with the goods on 'em – in the act of attacking. If I could once do that – Well! But why do you ask?'

'Just wanted to be sure, that's all.' Evelyn gave a shrug. 'If it should ever fall to my lot to be able to do anything I'll try and nail them in a bunch. Because I'm a woman it doesn't necessarily mean I'm scared of a bunch of ruffi-ans.'

Clayton rose. 'Better forget such notions,' he advised.

Evelyn accompanied him as far as the porch and gave him a final wave as he mounted his horse and cantered away toward the gates. Then she closed the door slowly and the troubled look Clayton had noticed returned to her face. Pensively she wandered back into the centre of the room . . . .

10

With the passing of a week, and then a fortnight, with nothing unusual occurring and no fresh clues to help him, Sheriff Clayton could be forgiven for losing something of his alertness. In fact he was almost prepared to believe that, knowing he would be watched henceforth, Dudley Stroud had given up all idea of trying to enforce the wishes of the Martin Oil Combine.

Certainly the lawyer had made no suspicious moves, nor were there any suspicious telegraph messages going back and forth. Whether or not there was anything going through the mails Clayton did not know, nor had he the authority to enquire.

Actually, Stroud had no need of either means of communication. All the necessary contacts he wanted were made through the clients who called upon him at intervals. Convinced from the prevailing peace that he had indeed shot Barry Ward dead, his new plans were forming, and at the end of the fortnight they had reached fruition. To Hank Andrews he gave final instructions.

'Tonight it will be the Sleepy V,' Stroud explained, as the puncher listened attentively. 'I'm leavin' it to you to pass the word on. We meet on the trail which goes past the Sleepy V spread; then we'll converge on the place.'

'OK, but I ain't at all sure about the sheriff. I got the idea him an' his men are watchin' us. How d'you figure dodgin' him tonight?'

Stroud grinned. 'What d'you suppose he'll do if there's a slap-up fight in the Long Trail saloon?'

'Tidy it up, I reckon. It's his job as sheriff.'

'You guessed it. That's why we're raidin' fairly early, round about ten-thirty, half an hour before the Long Trail closes. Get two of the boys to start somethin' there an' have somebody fetch the sheriff when things get out of hand. He'll have enough to occupy him for quite a time. The boys who start the trouble will probably end up in the hoosegow – at least for the night – but they'll be well paid for it.'

'OK – good as done,' Hank assented. 'But supposin' the sheriff ain't home – that he's roamin' around some place?'

Stroud shook his head. 'He won't be. He's got a duty to the town an' he can't be strayin' about just anywheres. The only ones likely t' be watching 'll be some of his men. If they are we'll settle them, same we'll settle that old fool Clint Morgan an' his old woman at the Sleepy V. Only two of 'em there to deal with, so it should be dead easy.'

The lawyer thought things out for a while, and then, evidently satisfied with his cogitation, he nodded.

'That's all, Hank. Pass the word round. We meet at ten-forty-five at the angle of the Sleepy V trail – and don't bungle things!'

Hank Andrews grinned and went out.

Exactly as he had ordered, at 10.45 Stroud, in dark shirt

and riding-pants, with a black sombrero and kerchief to his eyes, his .44 in its holster, was met at the angle of the trail by another eleven horsemen, kerchief-masked as he was.

'Everythin' fixed?' Stroud asked shortly.

'Everythin',' answered Hank Andrews. 'I reckon the Long Trail should be rarin' t'go right now.'

'Who'd you get to take it on?' Stroud enquired.

'Jed and Harry. An' they said they'd make it good even if they had to bust each other's heads with beer bottles.'

'They'd *better* make it good,' Stroud snapped. 'Now come on!'

With him in the lead the men spurred their mounts to action and, half a mile further on, turned suddenly from the trail across gently sloping grazing land. In a little depression, a dark square under the stars and almost surrounded by sycamore trees, was the Sleepy V ranch.

In a swift drumming of hoofs the twelve horsemen bore down swiftly towards the trees, drawing rein when they had passed beyond them and the ranch house was clearly visible against the stars. From a distant bunkhouse lights gleamed. The lower windows of the ranch house itself were also lighted, in which room presumably Clint Morgan and his wife were seated.

'I'll go ahead on foot,' Stroud murmured, 'an' see if I can talk sense into 'em. You stick around here, an' if any men come out of the bunkhouse you know what to do.'

He half turned, preparatory to slipping from the saddle, then he paused in mid-action as a gun suddenly exploded, a little distance in the rear.

Instantly the rest of the men swung round and stared, just in time to see the flash of flame and hear another revolver shot, at a point a little way beyond the ring of sycamore trees.

'Do you suppose it could be Barry Ward?' Hank Andrews gasped.

'Oh, shut up!' Stroud snapped. 'It *can't* be!'

The door of the distant bunkhouse had slammed open and men were running out into the night, inquisitive as to the shots. Lights also came up in the doorway of the ranch house.

'I'm gettin' out!' Hank decided, wheeling round his horse.

Stroud fingered his gun and as he too rode with the rest of his men he tried to sight his weapon on a dim figure on horseback beyond the sycamores. Then suddenly his horse, and those of his cohorts, stumbled helplessly, their forelegs buckling and throwing their riders.

It dawned on Stroud even as he toppled through the air that a rope had been fastened taut between the sycamore trees, low down, and the horses had fallen over it. Swearing, still holding his gun, Stroud tried vainly to aim at the single shadowy figure on horseback who was now moving at top speed amidst the struggling men and horses. As fast as each man got up the lash of a stockwhip cut across his neck and knocked him flat again. The horses, once up, galloped away in fright, nor did the lone horseman try to stop them.

Stroud got to his knees and waited until the figure on the horse came sweeping towards him. The aim he had intended was useless for this time the tail-end of the stockwhip struck clean across and coiled around his gun hand. With a gasp of anguish he dropped the weapon and gripped his flayed fingers tightly.

Dazed, he stared about him. Presently he picked his gun up again. He was just in time to see the horseman returning. This time no stockwhip struck. Instead something wet swooshed over him and his men, from a can. From the odour he identified it immediately as kerosene.

'Quick! Move!' he shouted frantically. 'It's *kerosene*!'

Those from the ranch and bunkhouse came upon the scene at this moment, but they checked themselves as a bundle of lighted papers sailed through the air, thrown by the black arm of the horseman. For a moment he was plainly visible, hat drawn down, hood-mask in position – then the lighted paper landed in the midst of the men and flared on the soaking oil. Shouting hoarsely they sprang to their feet, beating at their clothes.

'Run!' Stroud yelled. 'Run, for God's sake!'

He set the example, beating at himself as he went, and followed by revolver shots. He saw one man go down, another, but this was evidently all the ranchers were prepared to do. The shooting ceased and, the flames gradually being slapped to extinction, ten scorched, thrashed and bedraggled men crawled across the grazing land and looked vaguely round for horses which had vanished.

'That dirty coyote!' Stroud breathed venomously. 'I'll kill him for this – an' his sister too! He must have more lives than a wildcat. I must have missed him the other night . . . .'

He stared across the starlit pasture and then shrank back amongst his men at a sudden drumming of hoofs. For a moment a black rider was visible: a stockwhip exploded like a gun over the heads of the cowering men, then the rider had gone . . .

*

Towards noon the following morning the foreman showed
the sheriff into the living-room at the Sloping S ranch.
With a smile Evelyn got to her feet as Clayton came
forward, tugging off his hat.

'Glad to see you again, Luke. Please sit down.'

Clayton shook hands. 'Thanks all the same, Evelyn, but
I'm not stayin'. I can see you've work to do – An' say,'
Clayton broke off, in obvious concern, 'you're not lookin'
too good to me. What's the matter? Feelin' ill?'

'Ill?' Evelyn looked surprised. 'Why no! Never better.'

'Just wondered . . .' Clayton did not seem convinced.

The girl half reclined against the table and folded her
arms. Clayton's eyes went over her trim, womanly figure in
the light cotton frock. He found it hard to keep his mind
on business.

'I – er —' he hesitated. 'Mebbe you'll have heard about
last night's affair? Over at the Sleepy V?'

'No, I haven't. Was there another raid?'

'There was – which your brother completely smashed
up.'

The girl frowned. 'But my brother? Why do you remain
so confident that it is my brother, Luke?'

'Look, Evelyn.' Clayton took a step towards her, 'It can't
be anybody else but your brother because nobody else
would have the nerve, or the motive.' Briefly, he outlined
to her what had occurred.

'And you mean my brother did all that?' she asked
sharply.

'Most of it. Clint Morgan killed two of the men: he was
in his rights since he was shootin' down a trespasser. Your
brother didn't kill anybody. He used a stockwhip and a can
of kerosene and scattered the raiders' horses. Without

drawing a gun he got the mastery of the situation completely.'

'Then in that case he's behaving according to law, isn't he?' the girl asked. 'He's not done a thing for which you can arrest him.'

'I've no wish to arrest him,' Clayton responded. 'In fact, if only I could find him I'd congratulate him!' His eyes regarded the girl so steadily that she averted her gaze. 'Look, Evelyn, why don't you tag along with me?'

'I think we've been over this before,' she answered quietly. 'I've nothing more to add.'

Clayton sighed. 'All right, I can't force you. I —'

'Tell me something,' the girl interrupted. 'How did it happen that my brother broke up this intended raid – assuming it *was* him? I thought you were watching every movement of Stroud's?'

'I freely admit that he duped me.' Clayton looked rueful. 'I had to straighten out a brawl in the Long Trail saloon at the very time the raid occurred. Naturally the thing was arranged, to keep me busy. As for your brother, he must have been on the watch. He knows as well as any of us that there are only four likely places where the raids can occur. Anyway, the two men who were killed have been identified. They're just cattlehands, both of them belonging to the Roaring J outfit, and in the ordinary way they were good enough workers. In their off-time they evidently worked for Stroud.'

The sheriff was silent for a moment or two and then added, 'I can think of only one place where your brother might be hidin' out, Evelyn – and that's the mountain foothills. I've looked once and seen nothin', but I'm aimin' to go there again right now.'

'Supposing he *is* there,' Evelyn said. 'Why can't you leave him alone? He's helping the community. You admit that.'

'Sure I do, but I'm the sheriff, and *I* represent the law, not your brother.'

'It's ridiculous,' the girl protested. 'You are tied down by regulations; my brother is not. He can act freely.'

'Too freely, mebbe. Sorry, I have to interpret the law, an' I reckon I'll be on my way.'

Evelyn hesitated a moment and then made up her mind.

'I'll come with you. If my brother *is* in the mountains I'm as anxious as you are to see him. Wait while I change.'

Clayton nodded as she went into an adjoining bedroom. Idly he wandered outside and swung into the saddle of his horse. Ten minutes afterwards the girl reappeared in her riding-skirt and silk shirt. It was not long before she led a saddled pinto from the stables, climbed up on its back, then joined Clayton as he jog-trotted his mount towards the yard gateway.

'Where do you intend to start looking in a wilderness like this?' the girl asked him, looking about her in the torrid blaze.

Clayton nodded ahead. 'That central arroyo there. It leads straight to the mountain foothills.'

Evelyn's expression was half perplexed and half grim, as though she had been caught out by Clayton's decision to take the very route her brother had said he would take. That it was a natural decision, because of the topography of the landscape, did not occur to her.

'Everythin' else apart,' Clayton said presently, 'there's no reason why we can't maintain our friendship is there, Evelyn?'

The girl glanced in surprise. 'But we *are* good friends, surely? In fact *more* than that?'

'Well – I dunno.' Clayton grinned uncomfortably. 'I have the feelin' that you think of me now as a lumberin' officer of the law who keeps bustin' in where he shouldn't.'

'I never thought of you as anything of the kind. I haven't forgotten your courage back in Eagle's Bend, when you operated in what wasn't even your own territory. And from what I've seen and heard concerning you since I came back – mostly through my foreman Clem Hargraves, who ought to know – you're one of the most honest, conscientious sheriffs North Point has ever had. I admire you enormously.'

Clayton's uncomfortable grin became shy, even boyish. 'Well, I reckon that's mighty nice to know. And . . .'

He stopped talking suddenly and became a sheriff again. He and the girl had reached the central arroyo and drew rein. Silent, leaning on the saddlehorn, Clayton gazed thoughtfully into the distance towards the mountains.

'Reckon I was right,' he said at last, pointing. 'See for yourself. There's not only one horse's trail in this dry earth, but several – both comin' and goin'. We'd better follow this course right now.'

'Can if you like,' the girl assented. 'But the number of trails may be accounted for by the fact that I ride along here in the morning for exercise. Remember? You saw me coming back.'

'We'll follow the arroyo just the same,' Clayton said.

The various hoof-marks continued throughout the length of the old watercourse, vanishing eventually where the arroyo joined the stony ground of the mountain foothills.

Far away was a single genuine water-course, catching the sunlight, the only means of irrigation for the Sloping S pastures.

Clayton still jogged his horse onwards, gazing at the ramparts.

'Not much you can get out of this lot, is there?' Evelyn asked him presently. 'If my brother *is* in these mountains he might be just anywhere.'

'Not just *anywhere*, Evelyn,' Clayton corrected, shaking his head. 'You can't get much higher than the foothills in mountains like these, an' in the foothills are plenty of natural caves to hide in.'

The girl shrugged, keeping her horse behind Clayton's as he rode onwards and upwards steadily. When they had reached the top of a narrow acclivity Clayton drew rein again and he and Evelyn looked about them.

On three sides there stretched the whole territory, with the square marks of ranches and the town of North Point itself, a queer, doll's house affair at this distance, at the central focusing point. Far behind them now, the thread of a stream running towards it, was the Sloping S.

'There couldn't he a better spot than this for anybody to watch what's going on at the different ranches,' Clayton said.

He turned and surveyed the towering mountain wall to one side of them; then, slipping from the saddle, he inspected the pebbly ground of the acclivity. The girl remained on her horse, leaning on the saddlehorn and watching the sheriff's activities. A troubled light was in her violet eyes. For all the easy manner he adopted she knew nothing was escaping him.

At length he began examining the rough rock of the mountain wall. Then he gazed along the extremely narrow trail that marked the acclivity's continuation.

'Been a mount along here,' he said. 'A chestnut, too.'

The girl dropped from her saddle and came over to join him. Distinctly gleaming in the sun, caught in the roughed edges of the rock were horse-hairs.

'Chestnut,' Clayton repeated, and as the girl gave him an enquiring glance he added, 'Seth Edwards gave the stranger – your brother, I reckon – a chestnut mare on the night his spread was raided. This isn't coincidence. Let's go further.'

Leaving their horses tethered they moved slowly along the narrow pathway: it was little more than a ledge beside a 300-feet deep chasm. After following it for perhaps half a mile Clayton suddenly paused.

'Here's one of several caves,' he exclaimed, pointing. 'I've examined it before – but by night. Might as well try again now.'

He hurried forward the few remaining yards and plunged into the cave mouth. The girl followed him in slowly and looked about her. In the recesses of the cave she could hear Clayton moving about but could not see him – until the flare of a match and flickering yellow flame gave his whereabouts.

'Now I get it,' he murmured. 'Say – come here!'

The girl went over to him and he indicated a high wall of rock, then pointed behind it. There were empty meat cans, some neatly folded bedding, and the remains of animal feeding-stuff.

'Been used, and recently,' Clayton said, picking up one of the blistered and bent meat cans and tossing it down again. 'I missed this shielding wall last time.'

'Certainly *somebody's* been using this cave,' the girl agreed, 'but that doesn't say that it's my brother.'

'I'm satisfied that it is,' Clayton told her briefly. 'I don't expect to find him here but there's no doubt he heard us coming – or else saw us from that vantage point where we stopped, at the top of the acclivity. Now he must be hiding some place.'

He stepped out of the cave again into the sunlight, megaphoned his hands and shouted with all his power.

'Barry Ward! *Bar-ry*! Come out and talk! There's nothin' to fear . . .'

There was not even a suggestion of a response, except for the muttering, dying echoes of Clayton's own voice. He gave a shrug as the girl joined him.

'I've no time now to search for him,' he said briefly. 'Nor would I attempt it alone. But I'm coming back with some of my boys and if I search night and day I'll find your brother somehow.'

Evelyn said nothing. Turning, she wandered back along the pathway with Clayton behind her.

11

If anything were needed to make Dudley Stroud's temper any viler, an announcement in the latest issue of the *North Point Herald*, which appeared twice a week, did it. He had only been in his office an hour, the morning after the abortive raid on the Sleepy V, when the girl who delivered papers brought it to him. Morosely, he read, his expression darkening into fury.

AVENGING RANGER AGAIN ROUTS DESPERADOES!

Though the identity of the Avenging Ranger who is aiding helpless ranchers and the law to beat the sudden wave of crime and murder which has come to North Point remains obscure, this paper, on behalf of everybody in North Point trying to maintain order, takes this opportunity of expressing its profound gratitude.

Our sheriff, much respected though he is, is a busy man and cannot be expected to be everywhere. Last night, for instance, he was quelling a brawl in the Long Trail saloon at the very time the raid on Clint Morgan's Sleepy V ranch occurred, and but for the Avenging Ranger more murder and arson would undoubtedly have taken place.

Mr Morgan, in a statement, seemed more amused than alarmed by last night's incident. It seems that the Avenging Ranger, without firing a single shot at the attackers, only firing into the air to attract their attention, routed them completely by using a lariat, a tin of kerosene and a stockwhip. On the previous occasion, when they attacked Seth Edwards' B-bar-20 ranch, the Avenging Ranger took away one of the gunman's twin .44 guns, which shows how perfectly he knows what he is doing. There is one person in this town who is known to wear .44s, mentioning no names. Contempt and ignominy is what these ruffi-ans deserve – and it is what they will get until a rope is round their necks.

Stroud flung the paper savagely aside and jammed a cigarette in his mouth. He lighted it and then drew back his right shirt-cuff and looked at the red weal still on his hand where the lash of the stockwhip had struck with such fiendish effect.

'Good as accusin' me,' he muttered. 'An' I don't under-stand who this Avenging Ranger is, either. I could have sworn I pumped lead into Barry Ward. He ought to be as dead as carrion.'

Though he would not openly admit it, he had, he knew, reached the place where he just did not know what to do next. But as things worked out decisions were being taken for him, and they first became apparent the following evening.

He had just finished his evening's work at home upon a

legal matter and darkness was commencing to settle when a sharp rapping on the back door sent him to open it. A square-faced man with light-blue eyes was standing outside, his horse at the entrance to the yard. He was tall, dusty, attired in black sombrero, shirt and riding-pants. From the look of him he had come a distance.

'Deake Collins!' Stroud exclaimed in surprise, recognizing him – and a sense of uneasiness came upon him. 'I never expected to see you around North Point.'

'If it wasn't gettin' dark and I hadn't got a mighty good reason for being here you wouldn't see me now, either,' Collins responded.

'Come in,' the lawyer invited, and led the way into the living-room. 'You'll have a drink?'

'Whiskey,' Collins said, and threw himself into a chair.

'You've come a long way if it's from Karing's Head,' Stroud commented, handing a drink over and retaining one for himself.

Collins did not comment immediately. He downed the drink, put the glass on the table, then said sharply:

'Mebbe you'll understand better when I tell you that the big fellow has been havin' copies of the *North Point Herald* sent to him, and a statement in yesterday's issue points the finger at you and gives a lot of credit to an Avenging Ranger.'

'Oh – that!' The lawyer sat down slowly, contemplated his drink, and then finished it. 'It was exaggerated,' he said.

'The boss isn't lookin' at it that way. He's pointing to the fact that the paper says it's the second time this unknown has bested you. In fact the big fellow is sure burnin' up plenty over the fact that you've bungled every job so far – three all told.'

'So he sent you all the way from Karing's Head to tell me so?' Stroud enquired bitterly.

Not a muscle moved on Collins' lean, bronzed face.

'He sent for me, gave me my orders, and I'm here to carry 'em out. He's worked out a plan whereby you can nail this Barry Ward – and it's certainly him – once and for all.'

'All right, I'm listening,' Stroud said. 'What is it?'

'What's the name of your head man in this town?'

'Hank Andrews. Why?'

'Never mind.' Collins got to his feet. 'I can't explain this scheme in words, Stroud: I'll have to show you. Get your horse and come with me.'

A brief premonition of danger seized Stroud and then passed away again. Even if there were danger there was nothing he could do about it. Collins being directly under Emerton Martin in authority there was no alternative but to obey his orders.

'You're sure,' Stroud asked, as he led the way out of the living-room, 'that you weren't seen coming here?'

'Sure as can be, I reckon. Why?'

'Because the sheriff is watching my movements, and as you can tell from the paper I'm suspected.'

'Yeah,' Collins said. 'Which makes it tough for you.'

Once outside Collins vaulted into the saddle of his own mount and leaned indolently on the saddle-horn as he watched the lawyer saddling his horse in the little stable.

When at last he emerged with the horse behind him Collins led the way on to the pasture land, and then across it in a wide detour of the town.

Finally he bore leftwards so that he and Stroud travelled across the scrub land, and eventually to the mountain foothills. Here, in the gathered dark, Collins called a halt, the first words he had spoken during the entire trip. His voice was as level and unemotional as usual, and he added:

'Get off your horse, Stroud.'

The lawyer complied, puzzled and vaguely uneasy, his hand straying to the comforting pearl-studded butt of his solitary .44. He wished he still had the twin to it.

'Well, like I was sayin', the boss has a plan,' Collins said, gazing about him in the starlight. 'It's mighty simple. All that's needed is a new brain in control of North Point. Somebody who isn't suspected, like you are; somebody who isn't a sittin' target for the watchful sheriff and the Avenging Ranger.'

'What in blazes are you talkin' about?' Stroud demanded. 'I'm doing the best I can.'

'And it ain't good enough! Don't blame me, Stroud: I'm not the big fellow. I'm simply carryin' out his orders.'

'But this plan you spoke of —?'

'I told you: somebody else. Me, to be exact. In a few weeks I'll finish off this job you've bungled, and finish it off properly, too. *And* I'll wipe out this durned upstart Barry Ward. As for you, Stroud, you're off the payroll – and this is a nice quiet place to tell you so.'

'Why, you —' Stroud snatched out his gun as he caught the glint of starshine on Collins' own levelled weapon. They fired together, Stroud a couple of seconds behind Collins, and missing him as he dodged sideways.

Collins stood watching as Stroud slowly collapsed to the stony ground and became still. He waited for a moment or two and then he blew the wisping smoke from his gun barrel and holstered the weapon.

He stooped and picked up the .44 the lawyer had

dropped and examined it. Then he replaced it in the lawyer's holster. This done he turned and slapped Stroud's horse sharply across the withers, sending it scurrying in sudden fright towards the upper reaches of the foothills. His face as wooden as an image Collins climbed back into his own saddle and rode swiftly away, once again taking a wide, roundabout, detour, but eventually gravitating towards the fan of light which marked North Point.

It was close on an hour after dealing with Stroud that he entered the Long Trail saloon, to find it mounting to its usual night activity. He walked through the reek of tobacco smoke to the bar counter.

'Whiskey,' he told the barkeep. When it had been served him he leaned with one elbow on the counter, fiddling with the glass, and looking about the crammed, busy room.

'Passin' through?'

Collins glanced and found it was the barkeep talking.

'Yeah,' Collins assented. 'Matter o' fact I'm lookin' for a jigger by the name of Hank Andrews. Happen to know him?'

'Sure do. Over there.' And the barkeep nodded to a puncher at a distant table, sitting alone with a glass of beer.

Collins picked up his whiskey glass, walked over to the puncher's table and sat down opposite him.

'You Hank Andrews?' Collins asked brusquely, half emptying his glass and putting it down again.

'S'posin' I am?'

'You've gotten yourself a new boss in place of Stroud.'

The puncher straightened in sudden attention. 'How am I supposed to be sure? What happened to Stroud?'

'Never mind.' The light-blue eyes stared coldly across the table. 'All you've got to do is as you're told. When I want you where do I get in touch with you?'

'Right here. I'm here every evenin'. Too risky to send for me at my work. If I need *you* where do I look?'

'You don't. But if there's something vital,' Collins amended, 'I'll be at the Mountain Hotel.'

Hank Andrews swallowed a mouthful of beer. 'I still don't know if you're on the level. Y'might be a law officer.'

'If I was I'd clap you in jail pronto, and you know it. My name's Deake Collins. Some call me "Death's-head".'

'Collins!' The puncher's eyes widened. 'Yeah – sure. Now I come to think of it Stroud's mentioned you once or twice.'

'From now on,' Collins said, finishing his drink, 'I reckon there'll be action a-plenty – an' one of the first things we'll be dealin' with will be this Avenging Ranger who keeps nosin' in where he shouldn't.' He got to his feet and lighted a cigarette.

'You'll be hearin' from me,' he added, and turned to go. 'Tell the boys.'

Before he could reach the batwings, however, they opened and Sheriff Clayton came striding in. The look on his face clearly indicated he meant business.

'I want some of you men to form a posse,' he announced looking about him. 'It's the Avenging Ranger again.'

There was no immediate movement. Collins dropped his cigarette on the floor, heeled it, and waited. The talkative barkeep spoke.

'What's he done, Sheriff? He's on our side, ain't he? Judgin' by what's happened so far.'

'No doubt on it, but this time I think he's crossed with

the law and for that reason I've got to get him. One of my
men was near lawyer Stroud's house 'bout two hours ago
and saw a horseman ride up. Couldn't rightly see who he
was – it was gettin' dark – but since he an' Stroud went off
together towards the mountains, so fast my man couldn't
keep up with 'em, it looks more'n likely that the horseman
had Stroud at gunpoint an' he couldn't do anythin' but go
with him . . .

'I don't have to tell any of you, here,' Clayton went on
grimly, 'that we all know Stroud is at the back of these
ranch attacks – so what more natural than that the
Avenging Ranger finally decided to come and get him,
and finish off unfinished business?'

'I reckon that's natural enough,' a puncher agreed,
'but we ain't aimin' to corral a man who's doin' a mighty
lot o' good to this community. If he shoots Stroud, all th'
better! He's only doin' what any of us here'd do if we
didn't have respect fur the law.'

'Joe's right, Sheriff,' another remarked. 'There's such a
thing as stickin' too close to law sometimes.'

'Only because I've got to. I'm still asking for a posse.'

'I was ridin' the trail into North Point 'bout an hour
ago when I heard two shots,' Collins remarked, lounging
forward. 'They came from some spot up in the mountains.'

Clayton turned to him. 'You sure of this?'

'I reckon so. I don't know what it was all about, but it
does look as though there might ha' bin a little shootin'.'

Clayton eyed him. 'Stranger around these parts, aren't
you?'

'Yeah. The name's . . . Ted Smith. I'm here on cattle
business.'

Clayton nodded and turned back to the assembly.

'Well, since there's been gunplay I've got to find out what it's all about,' he said. 'How many of you are coming? Don't forget it may be that Stroud did the shooting and finished the Avenging Ranger. If so I'll have Stroud to bring in.'

'That's right!' a puncher exclaimed, jumping up. 'What are we waitin' for, fellers? It's our job to help th' sheriff!'

It was well after midnight when Sheriff Clayton and his posse of men, together with two deputies, came upon the sprawled body of Dudley Stroud in the mountain foothills. Near to him, evidently recovered from the first scaring start it had received, was his horse, head nodding and reins dangling.

'Yeah,' one of Clayton's deputies remarked, holding the lantern to the dead face, 'It's Stroud all right. And a bullet straight to the heart, too.'

'Think you can dig it out?' Clayton asked. 'I'd like to know the calibre.'

'I can try.' The deputy opened the smallest blade of his jackknife and went down on his knee, the rest of the men gathered about him, one of the men holding the lantern

'Here it is, Sheriff,' the deputy said finally.

'A forty-four,' Clayton mused, peering at it. 'That's mighty interestin'.'

'Forty-four?' repeated the other deputy, Dave Henson 'Same as this.'

He handed across Stroud's gun and Clayton examined it

'One bullet fired,' he said, 'but I don't think it could have been suicide – not with the gun bein' back in it holster. Besides, Stroud had no reason to commit suicide.

'What d'you make of it, then?' Henson asked.

'Stroud used to wear twin forty-fours,' Clayton told him. 'You all know that the Avenging Ranger took one of his guns from him. Your imagination can fill the gap, I reckon.'

'You mean that Barry Ward shot Stroud with the gun he'd took from him – and that Stroud fired too, only mebbe missed?'

'Somethin' like that. Mebbe it was Barry who put the gun back in Stroud's holster. Anyway it's a mighty pity that Barry had to turn to murder after all. Now's the time when I've no choice but to run him in.' Clayton put the lawyer's gun and bullet in his pocket. 'I'm leavin' it to you fellers to try and trace Ward if he's anyplace in these mountains. I'm goin' to try and get information another way. And this time I will. Meet me in my office in the morning.'

Half an hour afterwards, despite the lateness of the hour, he was banging on the frame of the screen door at the Sloping S. There was no response. Puzzled, he turned away at last and then at the edge of the porchway he stopped. A figure was standing at the base of the steps with his gun levelled.

'What do you want?' the gunman snapped.

Clayton gave a smile of relief as he recognized the voice. 'All right, Clem. It's only me.'

'Why, doggone! Sheriff Clayton!' Clem Hargraves came hurrying up the steps, holstering his weapon. 'I never expected *you* at this hour.'

'I want a word with Miss Ward, but I don't seem able to wake her. It's important, too.'

'Soon fix that,' the foreman said, and felt in his pocket for a key.

Unlocking the screen door and then the main door he went into the dark livingroom. Here he paused to light the lamp and then crossed to the adjoining door of the girl's bedroom. He knocked sharply.

'Miss Evelyn! Miss Evelyn, it's me – Clem. The sheriff's here and wants a word with you.'

There was no reply or the vaguest sound of movement.

'This is all-fired queer!' the foreman declared. 'Unless she's a durned sight heavier sleeper than you'd think. Door's locked.'

'Break it in,' Clayton ordered, in sudden anxiety.

As Hargraves hesitated, Clayton himself acted. Hurling his shoulder against the flimsy door he sent it flying back on its hinges and stumbled into the dark room beyond. All that was visible was the dim square of window with the deep, starlit violet of the night outside.

Clem Hargraves hurried across the living-room, picked up the lamp, and came back with it in his hand. The rays revealed the puzzling, even forbidding, fact that the bed had been slept in.

'I don't like this,' the foreman muttered, looking about him. 'I don't like it a durned bit! Somethin' queer, some place.'

He went to the window and examined it. It opened easily.

Clayton picked up the oil-lamp from the dressing-table and began a search of the room. There was no sign of there having been a struggle, and his intention to check for himself as to whether the girl had stopped to don outdoor clothes was prevented by finding the door of the built-in wardrobe securely locked.

'I just don't get it!' Clem declared, scratching his cheek.

'Do you suppose she was kidnapped, or somethin'? Or did she go out on her own? She could've, whether by the door – takin' the key with her – or by the window.'

Clayton looked at the door. There was no key in the lock.

'When did you last see her?' he asked thoughtfully.

'Getting' on fur midnight. She works late sometimes.'

'Well, there isn't any sense in trying to find her in the dark.' Clayton shrugged. 'I'll come back in the mornin'.'

'Don't make it 'til around noon, then,' the foreman said. 'Providin' she's back she goes fur a ride every mornin' from about seven till twelve.'

Clayton nodded reflectively. 'Yeah, so she does. Ever seen her go off on these mornin' rides of hers?'

'I reckon not. There's too much to do around the spread in a mornin' for us to be watchin' what Miss Evelyn does.'

'Surely she could hardly leave the ranch without you seeing?'

'She could if she took the back gate. The ranch house hides it from our view.'

'Mmmm,' Clayton mused. 'Well, I'll have to think about it. I'll be back when it's daylight. About this door . . .'

'I can soon fix that with a couple o' screws, son.'

'OK – thanks.' Clayton left the room, went across the adjoining living-room, and so out to his horse again.

He was pensive as he rode away.

12

Clayton arrived at his office early in the morning to commence sorting out the details of the killing of Stroud. Dave Henson had left a report to the effect that the previous night's search had led nowhere. Barry Ward had not been found. The body of the lawyer was now in the town morgue, awaiting examination by the local doctor.

Clayton had hardly got through reading the report before the deputy sheriff responsible for it arrived in person.

'Thought I'd better see if there's anythin' more you intend doin' about this business, Luke, before I get down to my normal day's work,' Henson explained.

'I don't see what we *can* do, Dave,' Clayton answered. 'You say you've searched the mountain foothills thoroughly?'

'Sure did – all of us, but there wasn't a thing, 'cept a cave with a high rock wall across its middle. It's one we've looked at before – only this time I found some beddin' and empty meat cans. But no trace of young Ward.'

'I know about that cave,' Clayton said quietly. Then he asked, 'You didn't see any sign of Miss Ward, I suppose?'

The deputy stared. 'Miss Ward? Why, no. Should we?'

'Possibly.' Clayton explained the girl's absence.

'That's mighty queer,' Dave observed, pulling at his ear.

'I wonder if it is?' Clayton murmured. 'Blood's thicker than water, Dave. It wouldn't surprise me if she went to keep a date with her brother in the mountains some place, never expectin' anybody would come during the night and find she'd gone.'

'Yeah, I reckon that's possible,' Dave admitted, thinking: 'If so, she an' him must have hid themselves mighty well. We saw no signs of 'em. What happens now Stroud's dead? Sort of puts that gang of hoodlums out of action, doesn't it? He was the leader . . .'

Clayton nodded. 'That's the way I look at it. The only thing I don't like is that Barry Ward was the one who had to take care of him. I've got to run him in now whether I like it or not. That's all for now, Dave: thanks for your help.'

The deputy nodded and went out of the office. Clayton sat musing, hat up on his forehead and his legs thrust out in front of him. Tight-lipped, he stared into space.

'It *can* only be Barry Ward who shot him,' he muttered at last. 'Ward must be alive or the gal wouldn't go like that after him – an' nobody else but Ward would have been likely to make Stroud ride all the way to th' foothills. An' the shots came from there because the stranger heard 'em . . .'

Clayton's brow furrowed a little at the remembrance of the stranger. In the stress of events he had forgotten all about him. Until now.

'I s'pose he could be a cattleman, like he said,' he mused.

As far as he could see there was nothing wrong in that.

Such visitors were common enough in North Point.

With a sigh he got to his feet and straightened his hat. He was convinced he could make no more moves until he had questioned Evelyn Ward, so, early though the hour still was, he went outside to his horse and commenced a leisurely ride to the Sloping S. When he arrived he found Clem Hargraves going about his work.

'She ain't turned up yet, Sheriff,' he said worriedly. 'Me an' the boys have bin watchin', but there's bin no sign of her.'

'I'll take a look for myself,' Clayton told him.

In a minute or two he had drawn clear of the ranch and had the open pastureland and plain in front of him, with the distant yellow scar of the central arroyo stretching back towards the mountains. When he reached it he considered the back-and-forth hoof-prints, raising his eyes to look along the sandy trail to its furthest end. Then he gave a start. In the far distance he was just able to pick out a figure in the brilliant sunlight, a figure approaching on horseback.

He smiled to himself and rode on slowly. The figure took on form and outline and resolved finally into Evelyn in her riding-skirt and silk shirt.

'Well, Luke!' she exclaimed, drawing rein and smiling at him. 'Nice of you to welcome me back.'

'Been for your mornin' ride?' he enquired pleasantly.

'Of course. You know I always take one.'

'Yeah. An' that makes it kinda queer. It must have been a long ride, from about one in the mornin' – or earlier – till now.'

'One in the morning?' the girl repeated, a look of confusion struggling on her features.

'I came to have a talk with you about one o'clock, Evelyn, and with your foreman's help I broke into your bedroom. Your bed had been slept in, but there was no sign of you.'

'That's right enough.' The girl sighed. 'I couldn't sleep. I got up and went for a long ride until I felt drowsy. I found a sheltered spot in the foothills and dozed there. It was full daylight when I awoke; then I started for home.'

Clayton smiled broadly and the girl gave him an angry look.

'What's the matter?' she snapped. 'Don't you believe me?'

' 'Fraid not, Evelyn. And I'll tell you what I *do* think. I believe this story of a mornin' ride each day is so much bunk. You invented it so that you could have a reasonable excuse to come ridin' into your ranch towards midday. I believe you go from the ranch most nights around one or two, slippin' out silently so your men don't hear you. You leave your bed lookin' as though it's been used – and for one reason only. In case anybody should try to speak to you – as happened last night.'

'Why on earth should I do that every night?' the girl cried. 'Anyway, I have to sleep sometime, don't I?'

'Nothing to stop you once you get to the foothills, or one of those caves – or even to that cave where the beddin' is. With your brother on guard you'd be safe enough. An' I'm not sure that you do get much sleep: as I told you you're not lookin' too well. Since you're healthy otherwise it could be lack of sleep.'

Clayton met the girl's level violet eyes and they were challenging.

'You mean,' she said deliberately, 'that you think I keep a nightly rendezvous with my brother. Is that it?'

'That's it. I don't expect you to admit it, an' I've nothin' against you for doin' it. I reckon I'd do the same for a brother of mine. But things have changed, Evelyn. Your brother's a killer! And I've got to get him!'

The girl started. 'A – a killer —?'

Clayton gave her the details; then she asked a question: 'About what time did all this happen?'

'Time? Oh, probably around ten or eleven last night.'

'What makes you think it was my brother?'

'One: because he was seen by one of my men, or at least a figure like the Avenging Ranger was seen callin' on Stroud, and later they both rode off into the mountains, so fast my man couldn't keep up with 'em. Two: later still I went with a posse to investigate and we found Stroud's body with a forty-four in his heart.'

'And how does that prove my brother did the shooting?'

'It doesn't *prove* it, but everythin' points to it, enough for me to want him for questioning. Stroud used forty-four guns: your brother took one of 'em when he saved the Edwards ranch. Stroud's remaining forty-four had lost one bullet – but he couldn't reholster his gun after shootin' himself. The answer is mebbe he shot at your brother and your brother shot him back – and killed him. He can perhaps prove self-defence. A stranger ridin' into town along the trail heard two shots from the foothills. I don't think there could be much more evidence . . .'

'All of which boils down to what?'

'That you know what your brother did and are hidin' him some place. He's got to prove he isn't a killer —'

'He isn't!' the girl protested hotly. 'It couldn't have been him because . . .' She stopped, biting her lip and looking away. 'Well, it just couldn't,' she insisted.

'An' that's all you aim to say?' Clayton asked quietly.

'That's all – except, who's this stranger you mentioned? The one who heard the shots?'

'A feller by the name of Smith. In town to do a cattle deal or somethin'. Never seen him before.'

'And whereabouts did you say you found Stroud's body?'

'Ways up in the foothills. Not very far from the top of that acclivity we followed.'

'And this stranger was on horseback?'

'Sure was. Been ridin' hard too, judgin' from the dust on him.'

'Then look here,' Evelyn said seriously, 'do you think that a man riding the trail hard and fast – with the noise of hoofs and bridle in his ears – could hear two shots from high up in the foothills? Three miles from the main trail? Sound travels *up*, remember, not horizontal, in the mountains.'

Clayton rubbed his chin and squinted into the sunlight.

'I never looked at it that way,' he confessed. 'You mean it looks as though the stranger might have done the killin'?'

'Anyway, it's possible,' Evelyn said decisively. 'You say that your man saw a figure resembling my brother. That isn't evidence. It could have been this stranger, and when the thing was done he came back into town, maybe circuitously to avoid being followed.'

'Then how do you account for a forty-four being used? The stranger wears thirty-eights. I saw 'em in his belt.'

'There wouldn't be anything to stop him buying a forty-four from somewhere, would there, and then ditching it – after the shooting? I know the bullet would not match the original forty-four gun, but since you can't find that gun it doesn't signify.'

Clayton grinned. 'I reckon you've the queerest, doggone way of twistin' things around, Evelyn.'

'I'm only using commonsense,' she answered quietly. 'You've got it firmly fixed in your head that my brother was the only person with the wish to kill Stroud. That's wrong! Everybody in town had that wish – though I don't think any of them would have done anything about it. But somebody else surely had an even greater wish than *anybody* to be rid of Stroud – the oil combine, for which he worked and for which he had only towering failures to show.'

'Now,' Clayton said, narrowing his eyes, 'it begins to make a bit of sense! Come to think of it, it was mentioned in one of the columns of the local paper that one of Stroud's forty-fours had been taken from him by the Avenging Ranger. Whoever killed Stroud – and let's say for the moment that it was the stranger – could have known that and planned to fix it so it looked like murder done by the Avenging Ranger. It was a perfect set-up for him – motive, everything, and it wouldn't take much imagination to guess that the Avenging Ranger probably hid in the hills. So he took Stroud there to make it look like the real thing.'

'How was this stranger dressed?' the girl asked quickly.

'Er – black shirt and pants, black sombrero.' Clayton stopped and snapped his fingers. 'In fact, except for the face-mask, the same sort of get-up your brother wears. Yeah, and about his build too.'

'Then you'll question him?'

Clayton shook his head. 'No. That would put him on his guard, and that's the last thing I want to do. I aim to

show him – if he *is* mixed up in this – that he can't get any
further than Stroud did before him.'

'If it comes to that,' the girl said, with a wry smile, 'there
is no credit attaching to the law for stopping these
outrages. It's been the Avenging Ranger every time.'

'I admit it. Your brother.'

'I said the Avenging Ranger.'

Eyes met and at last Clayton's bronzed face was smiling.

'Some day I'll have you figured right, Evelyn. I know
you're holdin' out on me, but there's nothin' I seem able
to do about it.'

That same evening Hank Andrews suddenly found Deake
Collins seated at his table in the Long Trail saloon.

'Howdy,' Hank murmured, taking a draught from his
beer-glass.

Cold eyes fixed him. 'You bin talkin'?' Collins asked.

' 'Bout what?' Hank stared.

'Everythin'! That damned sheriff's watchin' me every
bit as closely as he watched Stroud. I've seen him – and
when I haven't seen him I've seen men idling about suspi-
ciously.' Collins swallowed down whiskey savagely. 'I can't
make a single move without being followed. Who tipped
off the tinbadge, anyway? There's somebody around here
who's wise to everythin' – an' I've got to find out who it is
and rub him out.'

'That shouldn't be tough,' Hank commented. 'The
biggest cause of our worries is the Avenging Ranger. An'
that, as most folks know, is Barry Ward. I ain't sayin' how
much he discovers because I've no way of knowin' his
movements, but I will guess that he passes on all his information to his sister at the Slopin' S – an' she, I bet you,

passes it on to th' sheriff. She an' Clayton's mighty thick with each other. I see'd 'em now an' again.'

Collins meditated and meanwhile ordered another drink.

'There's probably somethin' in what you say,' he admitted, surprised that Hank was evidently not as dumb as he looked. 'If she gets too awkward she'll have to be eliminated.'

'That's kind of risky, ain't it?'

'Shut up! I'm in charge now, an' I don't intend to pull my punches. This oil business has got to be cleared up once an' for all, an' no tittle-tattlin' woman is goin' to stop it.'

Collins drank off his whiskey and became confidential.

'I've been lookin' around and weighin' things up,' he said, 'an' while I was about it I looked at the Falling H spread.'

'Uh-huh,' Hank agreed. 'We never got around to that one.'

'I know it – and the other three Stroud bungled. But the Falling H is goin' to be the first of the successes. Tomorrow night. It shouldn't be difficult with only Walt Bairstow, his wife and their daughter to deal with. Their outfit doesn't live on the ranch but in town here, which is a big help. We'll be free to act. Bairstow will be offered the same terms as Stroud used to offer, and if Bairstow and his wife and daughter get tough about it they'll be hanged in the orchard. Then, as in the case of the Slopin' S, the place'll be burned to the ground.'

Hank looked dubious. 'Pretty much the old routine, boss. An' what do you suppose th' sheriff'll be doin'?'

Collins set his jaw. 'Naturally he'd never fall for a decoy

a second time, like that fight Stroud arranged in here, so that bein' so we'll have to take open action and settle him first.'

'You mean – kill him?' Hank looked openly alarmed.

'No. I reckon that'd be goin' too far. A dead sheriff could bring a marshal in. Just lay him out for a while so's we can get busy. I'll attend to him myself, an' you and the rest of the boys have got to take care of Clayton's men – those so-called punchers he has loungin' around who are actually doing nothin' but keep their eyes open. I don't know 'em because I'm new to the town, but you do.'

'I know 'em by their first names,' Hank answered sourly.

'All right then. Tomorrow night I'm leavin' it to you an' the rest of the boys to deal with each one of them. I'll tail the sheriff and get him. When that's done we'll all meet separately on the northbound trail that leads past the Falling H. Eleven o'clock. OK?'

'Sure. I get it.' Hank finished his drink. 'But you've not taken into account our biggest menace – the Avenging Ranger. Except for actually knockin' out Clayton an' his boys your plan is the same as Stroud's last one. We dodged Clayton an' ran into the Avenging Ranger, an' he near burned th' hide offen us.'

'Those days are over,' Collins responded. 'If he turns up tomorrow night I'll shoot him dead myself – with extreme personal satisfaction. An' whether I do or not I'll be callin' afterwards on that sister of his and find out how much she's been talkin', and, if need be, I'll find out where her brother is hiding. She'll know.'

The puncher nodded as Collins got to his feet.

'Leave it to me, boss,' he murmured. 'See you tomorrow night, the Falling H, eleven sharp.'

'Right.' Collins nodded, and ambled away through the midst of the assembly to the bar. Here he ordered another whiskey and stood thinking. A slow, deep voice at his elbow made him turn.

' 'Evenin', Mr Smith. Gettin' acquainted with the town?' Collins found Sheriff Clayton was standing beside him, playing with his glass, his bronzed face gravely smiling.

'I've bin lookin' it over, sure,' Collins assented.

'So I noticed.'

Collins took up his glass then set it down again.

'I know you've never taken your eyes off me since noon today,' he said curtly. 'You an' your men have been trailin' me as if I were a criminal.'

'Just a precaution.' Clayton shrugged. 'There's plenty of nasty business goin' on in this town an' around it, Mr Smith, an' every stranger who comes in has to be checked up on.'

'I object to bein' thought a criminal!' Collins snapped.

'Mind if I tell you somethin'?' Clayton said, his voice pitched low so that the rest of the men and women around could not hear.

'Well?' Collins swallowed half his drink and put down the glass.

'You'd show sense if you got out of this town, and stopped out! Your name isn't Smith and you're not here to make deals in cattle. If you were you'd have made some moves by now to get your business fixed – but you haven't.' Clayton's eyes became hard. 'You're here for only one thing, I reckon – to carry on where Dudley Stroud left off.'

Collins measured Clayton as he waited.

'For a sheriff you should know better,' he commented eventually. 'Sayin' things like that without any proof is dangerous.'

Clayton only smiled. Inwardly he was satisfied. He had exposed his hand for only one reason, to satisfy himself that Evelyn Ward's guess about the newcomer had been correct. There was no longer any doubt. Collins' expression proved it.

'I'm not leavin' town, Sheriff, for you or anybody else,' Collins cried fiercely in sudden anger.

'Up to you. If you don't I'll dump you in jail for murder.'

'*Whose* murder? What in hell are you talkin' about?'

'The murder of Dudley Stroud. Somethin' you said to me last night can be used as evidence pointin' directly against you.'

Collins seemed to be thinking swiftly, probably trying to remember what he had said the previous night. Clayton watched him narrowly, his face hard and determined.

'I'll hand it to you, Sheriff, you play a good game of bluff,' Collins admitted. 'If you had evidence against me you wouldn't give me the chance to leave town.'

'You're not leavin' town,' Clayton assured him, taking out his gun and pointing it. 'I'm bookin' you right now on suspicion of murder, and if it does nothin' else it'll keep you out of mischief while an inquiry's held.'

Collins stood with a thin, half-sneering smile on his lips, venom in his pale eyes. Then with a movement so swift it was impossible for the interested watchers to follow it, his right hand flashed up and threw what remained of the whiskey straight into Clayton's face. The sheriff gasped and lowered his gun as the stinging spirit bit into his eyes.

In that split second Collins made one mighty dive, delivered a bone-cracking uppercut to the jaw of a man barring his way, and then flung himself through the batwing doors – to be instantly pursued by a mob of shouting men.

Blinking and rubbing his eyes, Clayton raced after them, found them in a dispersing crowd in the street searching the boardwalks and the sides of buildings; but evidently Collins had made good his escape into the night. Slowly, angrily, the men started to drift back into the saloon and up the steps to the swing doors.

'Reckon he got away, Sheriff,' one of the men said, as Clayton holstered his gun.

'This means one of two things,' Clayton said grimly. 'Either he'll get out of town and stop out – and it'll mean the end of that gang of hoodlums – or else he'll stick around, an outlaw, and war between banditry and the law will flare openly. From now on we've all got to be prepared for anything.'

'Look, Sheriff,' one of the men said, 'we know the four ranches that've got oil on 'em. If this guy and his trigger-men attack – as likely they will – it will be at one of the four ranches. Why don't we make the owners get out and we'll take their places?'

'Waste of time, Bill,' Clayton answered. 'I've suggested that already and the ranchers just won't shift. We can't do it that way. We can only wait and watch, see to it that our friend doesn't get his horse from the hotel stable, and do everything we can to smash any further raid attempts.'

13

Though Collins' getaway had seemed to the angry men tumbling from the saloon to have something magical about it, it had merely been the outcome of quick thinking on his part. The moment he had dived into the street he had turned sharp right round the side of the Long Trail and wriggled into the foot-wide space beneath the flooring of the place, since, like most buildings in North Point, the saloon was supported on wooden pillars to prevent it subsiding into sand.

Thus, worming his way forward in the dirt, Collins came to the point by the porch steps and listened, hearing every word. And there he remained, grim-faced and sweating, until he felt reasonably sure that he could make an effort to escape. He was glad of one thing: the information that the hotel stable would be watched, which would stop him getting his horse, so he took the only alternative.

He emerged from his hiding-place, dusted himself down, and then waited in the deep shadows at the side of the building until at length a lone puncher rode in, slipped from the saddle, and tied his horse to the hitchrail. Whistling to himself the puncher strolled into the Long Trail and vanished beyond the batwings. Collins waited for a moment or two, then he glided swiftly from his hiding-place, unhitched the horse's reins in a matter of seconds and swung into the saddle.

Spurring the animal into violent motion he went in a cloud of dust down the side alley and out on to the dry, scrubby land bordering the backs of the buildings. He dropped from the saddle again when he came to the back of a building proclaiming itself as Carter's General Store.

Gun in hand, he climbed the low paling-fence that surrounded the back garden and went swiftly to the rear door. Fiercely he knocked. After a moment or two old Adam Carter himself appeared, wondering, framed by the lamplight back of him.

'What the —'

'Get inside.' Collins interrupted him, pressing the muzzle of his gun into Carter's stomach. 'Quick!'

'But I . . . Yeah,' the store-dealer agreed, backing, his eyes popping. 'Sure thing.'

'One peep out of you and I'll blast your innards,' Collins warned. 'Pack me up some stuff in a bedroll. I want tinned foods, horsemeal, bread, three bottles of redberry wine, and some cookin' hardware. An' make it quick!'

Still going backwards and watched by his alarmed but motionless wife and daughter, Carter went into his closed shop.

'Draw the shades and light the lamp,' Collins ordered.

Carter was too scared to try and pull a fast one. He tugged down the shades and secured them, lighted the oil-lamp, then began to fill a huge paper carrier with all manner of edibles as Collins selected them.

'Okay,' Collins said finally. 'Put the lot in a bedroll —'

'What about payin' for this stuff, stranger?'

'The only pay you'll get if you dare open your mouth about this is a slug in the belly. Shut up and do as you're told.'

With trembling hands Carter followed out orders. When at last the bedroll had been duly packed and roped up long-and-cross, Collins took it and went backwards from the store, slamming the rear door. He reholstered his gun and, supporting the bedroll on his shoulder, he leapt into the saddle, dug in the spurs and set his stolen gelding darting away under the stars.

He kept on riding until he came to the mountain foothills. He had a double purpose in coming to them. The chief one was the shelter they could give him, together with almost unassailable security; the other was the possibility that he might meet the Avenging Ranger somewhere – and dispose of him.

Without mishap he finally reached the main acclivity that Clayton and Evelyn Ward had followed together. There was no coincidence in the happening. There simply was no other safe way to reach the higher ramparts of the mountains.

At the top of the long acclivity Collins drew rein and looked about him, impressed by the panoramic view. The lighted windows of the various ranches scattered about the region gleamed like distant fireflies, only outclassed by the more flamboyant glow from the town of North Point itself.

'Reckon there should be plenty of chance to watch things when the daylight comes,' he murmured, jogging the horse on again as he searched for shelter.

He came upon it almost immediately: the cave which the girl and Clayton had examined and which, though Collins did not notice the fact now in the darkness, had the rock screen and behind it the old meat cans and bedding.

Dismounting, Collins looked about him, debating what he should do with his horse. Eventually he took it into the cave with him. It was safer than having it outside in case anybody happened unexpectedly to come along the lone mountain trail.

Collins unpacked his bedroll, opened it out on the cave floor, smashed up a tin of food with his jack knife, then cut a hunk from the loaf. He settled himself to eat, in between draughts from one of the bottles of redberry wine. He would have preferred coffee but circumstances did not permit it. When he had fed the horse he frowned in annoyance.

'Water . . . Reckon you can't do without water. Forgot that.'

He picked up one of the cooking-cans and peered outside. Everything was as quiet as before. Satisfied, he moved into the centre of the pathway and listened again, not quite sure whether or not he could detect the rushing of water.

He began to move in its direction, a distance of perhaps a quarter of a mile, and the sound grew unmistakably louder. Eventually he came suddenly upon a stream cascading down the mountainside from melting snows far up the heights.

He washed his face and hands whilst he was about it, then with the can filled with water he returned warily along the path, watchful all the time, never quite sure of what might happen next . . .

He stopped dead, flattening himself against the wall. Ahead of him had come a sudden sound of horse's hoofs coming towards him from the direction of the distant acclivity. He put down the can of water and drew his guns, waiting. Though the starlight was none too bright he presently descried a lone horseman just outside the very cave he had taken over. Even as he watched the horseman slid from the saddle and vanished in the cave entrance.

Collins gave a grim smile to himself. This was too easy! Guns in hand he tiptoed forward, reaching the cave just as the new arrival came out of it. Evidently he had discovered the various evidences of tenancy for he glanced up and down quickly, the face visible as a white blur.

'Reach!' Collins snapped.

The figure twirled round, hands rising in obedience. Collins stood where he was, none too anxious to reveal his own identity. He could just distinguish the lone horseman's broad-brimmed hat, haze of a face, dark clothes and slim figure.

'Avenging Ranger, huh?' Collins asked coldly. 'Or should I say Barry Ward?'

There was no answer. The figure remained with hands upraised.

'Too scared to talk, eh?' Collins questioned sourly.

This time the only response was what could have been interpreted as a clicking of the teeth – no more. At least that was how it sounded to Collins. Then a moment afterwards he realized how wrong he was when his stolen horse came suddenly out of the cave, drawn by the call, and planted itself between him and his captive.

'Outa the way, you hulkin' big cayuse!' Collins yelled in explosive fury, but those few seconds had lost him his advantage.

The Avenging Ranger swung, vaulted into the saddle of

his mount, and was gone along the pathway in a rattle of stones, grey dust rising into the starlight. Collins aimed his guns, then thought again about firing them. It would be a waste of good bullets. Furiously he reholstered them and glared at the silent horse.

Collins slept only fitfully throughout the night, his mind constantly stretched into alertness for fear of sudden attack – but nothing visible appeared. He was thankful when the dawn came, piercing the gathered mists of the night in blazing golden bars of sunlight. It made him feel safer.

After he had breakfasted and fed and watered the horse, he saddled it and then rode back along the rocky pathway to the end, from where it was possible to gain that all-encompassing view of the town of North Point, the plain, and the ranches.

Smoking idly and leaning on the saddlehorn, he contemplated the peaceful scene. Nearest to the mountain range was the Sloping S. He could make out the moving mass of cattle in the corrals and the tiny dots of men as they went about their work. Of Evelyn Ward he could see no trace, perhaps because it was too early. When eventually he did see her she was riding across the plain from the direction of the mountains, her dark hair flowing in the wind and her silk shirt and riding-skirt just distinguishable.

'Now what's that dame been doing?' Collins muttered to himself. 'Havin' words with that precious brother of hers, like as not. I reckon I've perhaps got his headquarters and he had to change fast. In that case she'll know where he is, and if there's any funny business tonight she'll talk – and plenty.'

When night came again he set off down the trail to the foothills. Once or twice on the way he paused, convinced that he could hear a horse's hoofs following him. He stared intently into the starshine but failed to detect anything. . . Of course it could have been the whispering echoes of his own horse's hoofs, yet somehow . . .

During the ride he detoured several times, never once giving the impression that he was heading towards North Point, but he reached it just the same in the finish – from an easterly direction. By this time he had his kerchief pulled well up over his face and his hat-brim drawn down.

At this hour of night the life of North Point was nearing saturation. The first stragglers were already coming out of the Long Trail saloon. Collins dismounted from his horse in the narrow alley between two buildings, and waited until one of the stragglers, a lone cowpuncher, came his way. Darting out, Collins seized the man and dragged him backwards, digging a gun in his back.

'Where do I find the sheriff?' Collins whispered. 'Where's his home?'

'At the far end of th' street – but I reckon you won't find him there. He's out on the prod for you some place. You're Smith, ain't you – the jigger he's a-lookin' for?'

'*Where's* he proddin' for me?' Collins snapped.

'I dunno exactly, but I reckon he's got men watchin' all th' trails leadin' frum town.'

'OK,' Collins responded briefly. Raising his gun he brought the butt down with smashing impact on the puncher's skull. Without a sound he crumpled and lay still in the dust.

Whirling back into the saddle Collins spurred his gelding and raced out of town behind the buildings, picking up the trail again a mile further on, the trail that in due course led past the Falling H ranch.

Once he gained the beaten track Collins began to move more warily, ever watchful, one of his guns drawn. It was not long before he caught sight of a distant blur of dark across the road in the distance. He dismounted swiftly, found a rock to which to tether his horse, and then crept along silently on foot, at times dropping into the dry grass which skirted the trail edge.

'. . . an' I reckon that with all these points watched he'll not get away, Sheriff,' a voice was saying, carrying clearly on the still air. 'The Falling H is surrounded.'

Collins narrowed his eyes and thought swiftly. This was the very spot where he had planned to meet his hench-men, and occupying it were Sheriff Clayton and his two deputies, astride their horses, peering into the night. With this point made clear it would not matter how many others were covered because from here to the Falling H it was a straight run across grassland to the orchards and the ranch itself.

Collins hesitated no longer. He drew out his other gun, then stepped out, on to the trail.

'Get off your horses, all three of you! You're covered!'

Clayton and his deputies swung round and saw the dim figure below them, starshine glinting on the gun barrels. They had more sense than to argue.

Clayton dropped down into the dust of the trail and his two deputies followed suit, their hands raised. Stepping forward, Collins took their guns from the holsters and threw them as hard and as far as he could into the dark-ness.

'How far do you reckon this is goin' to get you, Smith?'

Clayton snapped. 'Gettin' out of hand, aren't you? If we don't get you now we will later.'

'I'm goin' on trying,' Collins retorted. 'This fight isn't a secret any longer, Sheriff, it's open war – me and the men who work for me against you and that outlaw Barry Ward. An' he's alive, by the way. I've seen him.'

'Yeah?' Clayton questioned interestedly, but Collins did not satisfy his curiosity.

'I'll get all the four ranches Stroud tried to get, in spite of you, Sheriff —'

'Not while I've got witnesses right here listenin' to what you're sayin' you won't!'

'You'll never get me, Clayton: I'd kill you first. As for me gettin' the ranches, it isn't so crazy as it sounds. If I don't get the signatures selling the property I'll burn 'em to the ground, and th' occupants'll be taken care of so's they can never say who did it. After that, you and nobody else can stop the property being bought up, or leastways the land that's left. It won't be me that'll buy, naturally, but a stranger.'

'In the pay of the oil combine?' Clayton asked cynically. 'And the stranger will sell it to them?'

'Right! But you can't do nothin' about that. You'll have no proof, no anythin'. I'll be paid an agreed sum and then go.'

Collins stopped talking and glanced back down the trail. A party of some half-dozen horsemen was coming into view in the starlight. He waited intently, not quite sure whether they were Clayton's men or his own. As they came nearer and he saw the kerchiefs up to their eyes he breathed more freely.

'Tie these men an' gag 'em!' he ordered curtly. 'An'

hurry it up. There's other men around some place, watchin'.'

'Y'mean there *was*,' one of the newcomers answered drily. 'We've been busy takin' care of 'em, like you told us. We've got eight of 'em laid out, all told.'

'You didn't have t' use your guns?' Collins demanded. 'The noise of 'em would —'

'Nope. Just slugged 'em, good an' hard. Wasn't diffi-cult.'

Clayton had plenty he would have liked to say at that moment but he did not get the chance. A rough gag was jammed in his mouth and tied tight, then his wrists were fastened behind him, the cords being carried down to his ankles and secured there. When his two deputies had been treated likewise all three of them were lifted and dumped in the prickly grass at the side of the trail.

'OK, it's time we got busy,' Collins snapped. 'Get my horse from back up the trail yonder, one of you.'

A puncher obeyed the order and Collins holstered his guns. As his horse was brought for him he leapt into the saddle. Then, leading his ten men, he swept across the pasture land towards the dim bulk of the Falling H ranch.

'Stay here,' Collins ordered, when they all came beyond the orchard. 'I'll do the talkin'.'

The men waited, glancing anxiously about them as Collins strode up to the porch and thundered on the door. They saw the door open, and he entered. Presently he reappeared, forcing before him at the point of the gun the middle-aged owner of the ranch, his wife, and a woman of perhaps twenty-five. They were clearly visible in the oil-lamplight streaming from the ranch house living-room.

'You've only yourselves to blame for this,' Collins

snapped. 'I just can't figger why you're so plain obstinate when you can have a cheque for your signature right now. Since you won't, the three of you are goin' to hang.'

'You'll not get away with this, whoever you are,' Bairstow retorted. 'An' just *who* are you, anyway? It used to be Stroud who terrorized the neighbourhood, but I reckon it can't be him now – not that it makes any difference. The Avenging Range —'

'There'll be no Avenging Ranger this time,' Collins snapped.

He forced the three down the steps of the ranch porch and the cowpunchers slid from their horses.

'The orchard,' Collins said. 'Bring three lariats.'

His order was obeyed and without raising any further protest the rancher and his wife and daughter walked on until they came amidst the thickly-foliaged trees surrounding the ranch. Here, at Collins' command, they stopped. He looked about him.

'I reckon this tree's as good as any,' he said, as his men gathered round him. 'There's a low limb here.'

The three captives watched helplessly as ropes were thrown over it. 'Take the gal first,' Collins said. 'Mebbe when she starts swingin' her old man'll get some sense in his thick head.'

A puncher seized on the struggling girl firmly and dropped the noose of the nearest rope about her neck. Then the puncher glanced upwards sharply as there seemed to be a sudden wind rustling through the foliage.

'What was that?' he asked uneasily.

'What was what?' Collins demanded.

'I thought th' leaves of th' tree moved.'

'Aw, shut up! What else d'you expect with that rope

movin'? String the gal up and stop bellyachin'.'

'Yeah, sure . . .' The cowpuncher hesitated, then he added, 'The rope don't go up as far as the leaves . . .'

Collins set his jaw and peered into the dense foliage. He drew out his guns and angled them upwards.

'Come down from there, feller,' he ordered, 'before I blast the daylights outa you. I don't know how you got there, less it was by jumpin' from tree to tree from the end of the orchard. Yeah, I reckon you could ha' done it that way . . .'

Out of the leaves there suddenly dropped a lithe figure in black, whirling a heavy stockwhip. The astounded Collins' guns were lashed out of his hands in a second.

The next thing that Collins and his men, bunched together as they were, became aware of was white-hot lashes flaying them across their backs and faces: mercilessly, savagely, flattening them to the ground before they could even use their guns. They clawed the earth and shouted hoarsely.

One by one they struggled up and pursued by the searing lash, blundered away from the orchard and the ranch. It was only by degrees that they realized the onslaught had stopped. Pain biting into their limbs they raised their heads. The night was silent. The Avenging Ranger had gone. Collins mopped his sweating, bleeding face.

'I don't see you doin' much better'n Stroud did!' one of the punchers told him viciously.

'You shut up!' Collins turned and waited as another puncher came limping up from the direction of the orchard.

'Hosses have gone,' he announced bitterly. 'Been scared off, I reckon. Just like happened last time – and we'd best get out of here,' he added. 'Next thing we know the Avenging Ranger'll have released the sheriff and he'll be after us.'

'That's possible,' Collins admitted, his voice quivering with fury. 'Otherwise I'd go back an' finish those three like I meant to.' He came to a sudden decision.

'You'd better start lookin' for the horses. I've got other things to do. I'm goin' straight to the Slopin' S to get the truth outa that Ward girl. It ain't so far from here. I'll get that brother of hers if it's the last thing I do!'

He turned, his pains subsiding, and strode off into the night, leaving the men to do the best they could. As he strode on across the grassland he figured out what must have happened. He had been followed, even as he had suspected. Barry Ward had evidently seen what was about to happen – that a necktie party was on the programme – and had then climbed into the trees on the outermost edge of the circle and worked his way inwards from tree to tree until he had discovered which one was going to be used.

'Which isn't straight fightin'!' Deake Collins muttered savagely.

Scowling, he continued walking, across the rough ground and pasture land, until at last he came within sight of the Sloping S, dark and silent in the starlight. Now he began to move like a shadow, taking care to keep well away from the bunkhouse where he judged, correctly, that some of the Sloping S men might be on the alert. Without a sound he prowled until he came to a side-window of the main living-room. It was closed and locked but the blade of his penknife made short work of it.

He slid up the sash, climbed into the room and stood listening in the dark. There were no sounds. When at length his eyes were adjusted he headed towards the deeper black oblong of a connecting door and pulled at it gently. Nothing happened. He hesitated, then knocked sharply. From within came a mumbling voice.

'Yes . . . What – what is it?'

Collins smiled grimly, flung up his foot and kicked the door open.

'Don't move!' he ordered, staring at the dim shape in the bed under the window.

'What . . . Who is it?' gasped Evelyn Ward's voice.

'Somebody who's goin' to make you start talkin'. That infernal brother of yours upset all our plans again tonight an' I'm goin' to find out where he's hidin'. I know it's in the mountains some place an' I know you can tell me exactly where that place is.'

'And you really think I would?' Cold contempt had come into Evelyn's voice now.

'Yeah, I do! Get up!'

There was a short pause, then the girl obeyed, and became dimly visible in pyjamas. Collins waited whilst she reached for a gown and flung it about her.

'Well?' she asked curtly, and the answer was a blow in the face which sent her spinning against the wall.

'Talk!' Collins breathed, moving closer to her

Two more vicious backhanders hit her then Collins stopped abruptly at a sudden rush of feet in the living-room. He swung to the door and whipped round his gun.

'*Look out!*' Evelyn screamed in warning.

A second too late Collins fired, just as a gun blazed from the bedroom doorway. Collins' weapon clattered from his hand and he dropped on his knees, lurched and fell flat.

Evelyn sped swiftly out of the room and returned in a moment with an oil-lamp. Sheriff Clayton was holstering his gun and staring at the fallen figure.

'I reckon that takes care of him,' he muttered.

Evelyn nodded, her face pale and red-marked where the blows had struck her. Then she turned as a key rattled in the main door of the ranch. Clem Hargraves with two of his men came in.

'What – what goes on?' he asked blankly. 'Heck, it's the sheriff!'

'Take this body to my headquarters,' Clayton said, rising from the fallen Collins. 'He's dead. He was wanted for murder, anyway.'

Hargraves nodded and Collins was hauled out of the room.

Clayton looked at the girl seriously. 'I s'pose he was tryin' to find out where your brother is,' he said.

'Yes.' Evelyn rubbed her smarting cheeks. 'I don't know what would have happened if you hadn't turned up. How did you guess?'

'Not a matter' of guessin'. I was *told*. That brother of yours has been mighty busy tonight. He wiped out another raid attempt at the Falling H, and once again he didn't use a gun. Then he came ridin' up and released me and my two deputies. We were caught nappin' earlier on by Smith. Anyway, we found Smith's men so disorganized as they were lookin' for their horses that we got all of 'em. I made one of 'em tell me where Smith was and when I heard he was walkin' over to knock the truth out of you I came straight over.'

'Which means this murdering gang is finally smashed up?'

'Sure does,' Clayton assented. 'Your brother can come into the open now. I'm satisfied he didn't murder Dudley Stroud. Just tell me where Barry is and I'll go tell him.'

An odd look crossed the girl's face. Instead of answering, she asked a question. 'What about Emerton Martin?'

'He's sunk,' Clayton answered grimly. 'I'll have to explain to the Austin authorities about Collins' dead body. They'll look into it, and I'll guarantee the information they'll find will prove he was a go-between for Martin. They'll tie bows on Martin that'll put him away for the rest of his life . . . But I'm asking you again, Evelyn – *Where's Barry?*'

The girl looked at him with her violet-blue eyes. With a pang he recognized that light of sadness he had seen there once before.

'Dead,' she answered, her voice low.

'But he *can't* be! I saw him tonight —'

'You saw *me*,' she said. '*I'm* the Avenging Ranger!'

Clayton gave her a long incredulous stare and then sat down heavily.

'You! But how in heck —'

'Let me explain,' Evelyn said quietly. 'My brother came to see me after saving the B-bar-20 ranch and I promised to take him some food and supplies into the foothills. I did so, and found him dying. It was Stroud who had shot him. He knew it was. He died in my arms . . .'

The girl sat down slowly biting her lip over bitter memories. A tear welled in the corner of one eye.

'I buried him instead of advising you of the facts because, I asked myself, why should the good work he had started – to defeat those hoodlums – be allowed to collapse? I owed it to his memory that it shouldn't!' She looked at Clayton challengingly.

'Go on,' he said quietly.

'I resolved to take his place wearing his clothes and hood-mask, and using his horse. I'm fairly tall for a woman; he was rather short for a man. I believed that in the dark – and never speaking in case my voice gave me away – I could succeed. You'd taught me how to handle a stockwhip when we were in Eagle's Bend. I decided to use one instead of a gun.

'Naturally I had to pretend that my brother still lived because I knew that you, and the rest of the menfolk in town, would very soon have stopped my game otherwise. You would never have thought a woman capable of such things . . .'

'And then?' Clayton urged, smiling seriously.

'It was pretty hard going for me,' Evelyn continued. 'Every night I slipped out of here in disguise, taking care so as not to disturb Clem and his men, and went into the foothills, using the cave in which I had found my brother – the one you discovered later with the bedding in it. From that cave, every night, I kept watch on the plains below. That was how I kept in touch with the hoodlums' moves, with a pair of strong field glasses to aid me. By night I never slept, but I made up for it from dawn until mid-day in the cave, when I knew no raids could occur. Then I would change into my own clothes, put away my "Avenging Ranger" outfit in the saddle-bag, and come riding back to the ranch just as if I had started out, early in the morning, and returned around noon.'

Clayton gripped her arm. 'If only you'd told me, Evelyn! I would have understood.'

'No.' She shook her dark head. 'I'm sure you wouldn't. Or if you had you'd have been so afraid for me you'd have upset my plans somehow. It was a relief when you finished Smith – or whatever his name was – tonight, though I did see him up in the mountains and only just dodged him.'

'You did! Why didn't you tell me? We could have got him.'

'Because I was sure he'd have got you first. I'd put him on alert and after that anything could have happened. Besides, I wanted to finish my job properly. Call it bravado, call it inherited Western toughness, but that's the way I wanted it. You told me back in the hotel when I first arrived back that my father and brother had been proud of me when you showed them that newspaper. I felt I owed it to their memory to see their faith in me wasn't misplaced.'

'It certainly wasn't.' Clayton shook his head, inwardly marvelling at the girl's courage. He wanted to hold her, to kiss her, but he still had a further unresolved question.

'One thing more,' he said. 'About that tin of kerosene with which you set those men on fire . . .?'

Evelyn smiled faintly. 'I had a small cooker up in the cave for making coffee, and a can of kerosene. It occurred to me when I saw what was threatening at the Sleepy V that I could turn the kerosene to good use, and I did.'

'I just wondered,' Clayton nodded. 'And as for tonight I suppose you got back here before Smith – Collins – reached you ?'

'Yes,' the girl nodded. 'He was on foot, remember. I had time to get into bed. It's as simple as that, Luke, and now it doesn't matter if I become plain Evelyn Ward again.'

Clayton shook his head and the girl looked at him anxiously.

'You can't do that, Evelyn. The whole town needs to

know about your courage. I think the mayor ought to give a public vote of thanks to the Avenging Ranger.'

'I'd – I'd really much rather —'

'I'll have a word with him tomorrow about it,' Clayton added, grinning. 'You're not going to creep away after what you've done! Hell, no! And – and then . . .' Clayton's voice slowed and hesitated. 'And then I suppose you'll be hittin' the trail again for the school in Eagle's Bend?'

'No,' Evelyn answered. 'If I ever returned to teaching, I could do it equally well from here. Besides, coming back to these open spaces where I was born has really done something to me. I want to stay here and build the ranch up into something prosperous. It's what Dad and Barry would have wanted.'

'In that case,' Clayton said, his voice becoming deliberate, 'I don't think you ought to stay as plain "Miss Ward". Too durned dangerous. Besides, there are lots of things to be done – man's work; and old Clem Hargreaves can't look after *everything*.'

'What you really mean,' Evelyn said archly, 'is that I should become Mrs Luke Clayton, isn't it?'

'Yeah!' Clayton declared defiantly. He swept her into his arms, and looked into her eyes. He experienced another pang as he realized they were once again smiling. The shadow he had seen there had been lifted.

'I'd have asked you long ago only I didn't know which way you were goin'.'

'You know now,' she said.